Destiny

FOREVER & ALWAYS

BOOK ONE

CINDY SPRINGSTEEN

Copyright © 2015 by Cindy Springsteen

NEW EDITION

Printed in the United States of America

Cover & Book Design: Wicked Muse

Photo: Cindy Springsteen

New Edition Editor: Leanore Elliott

ISBN-10: 1530027624
ISBN-13: 978-1530027620

DEDICATION

This book is dedicated to two very special people: my Mom and Dad, who sadly aren't here anymore. Not a day goes by that I don't think about them and wish that they were still here with me on earth. I would have loved for them to have been a part of all the happiness life has brought me. The love they had for me impacted me in so many ways. There aren't enough words in the world to describe how much I love and appreciate all they did for me and my family.

Love and miss you Mom & Dad!

ACKNOWLEDGEMENTS

I never thought I would see my novel truly come to life a second time and be published again. It took a lot longer than I thought it would and I continue to learn in this process. So many people have helped me in this journey and in bringing this book back to life. It is very hard to know where to even start.

First a HUGE thank you to my family, my wonderful husband and two amazing children for supporting my writing career. They believe in my story and in me, more than I do at times. It has been a long hard road making this the best that I possibly could. Thank you all for standing by my side, Forever & Always!

Thank you my wonderful editor and cover designer, Leanore Elliott, who read this story over and over, to make sure it was as perfect as it could possibly be. Then you took so much time working with me creating a cover that everyone loves! I am blessed to have found you!

To Crystal Bozeman Clifton, my dear friend, who for the last five years has listened to me talk about this story and is always there to lend a helping hand or an ear to listen whenever I need it. You are a treasure and I am eternally grateful!

To Deborah Schmidt, Elizabeth Tencza, and Debra Delakas. Each of you made such impacts in my life and my choices. You have stood by me after all these years and continue to support everything I do! Love you!

To Micaela and Barbara Kessler, Lori Lite, Ella Gram, Mary Ann Robinson Meyer, Carol Ann, Debbie Pesiri Falcon, Krystle Javier, Maria Regina-Walters, Cheryl M Maye Pav, Jessica Baker-Bridgers, Belinda Gallant, Corry Parnese, Linda Phillips and so many more for always being there when I need you. Each of you plays a part in my inspiration to continue to write more.

To Air Supply, after approximately 34 concerts to which I have had the pleasure of attending, including the one where my children got to sing on stage with you. For 40 years, I have been listening to your music and I wanted to thank you! Your music inspires me always has and always will. Your songs are truly my story!

Prologue

A peaceful evening can take a turn in a split second. I have been anticipating this moment all week. I pour a cup of coffee and pick up the book I've been trying to finish. I sit on the couch and finally have time to relax. The television is on with the volume down low. It's been hard lately, to find time to enjoy the simple things in life.

From outside, a car door slams, then another, as angry voices filter in from the street. Waiting for them to stop, I pick up on my daughter's distinctive tone. I can't make out the words, but I feel the desperation. Moving to the window, I peek past the blinds. I see her out in the street, arguing with him, again. It's hard not to get annoyed, as this is the second fight this week. Will they wake up the whole neighborhood? I want to listen, but know I shouldn't. I don't want to interfere, but know that I might have to.

It is so hard to walk away and go back to the couch. As a parent, my every instinct is to protect my daughter. It takes every ounce of willpower to let her walk her own path. I stare at the pages of my book, unable to focus or read. The yelling continues as I try to block it out.

I believe some people are destined to be together. Then there are relationships that look like they will last forever, while fate works to intervene. My heart breaks for the pain of my daughter's unknown future.

Thirty-four years ago, I was that young girl on this same street. I was the one crying and begging for it not to end. I close my eyes and can still picture the scene as clearly, as if it happened just yesterday.

I remember everything about that night, that moment in time. I remember his face and the sadness in his eyes that I had never seen before, even having known him for so long. I was scared, I knew whatever he was about to tell me was worse than anything my mind could have imagined. It would forever change my life, as I knew it. The day when the person you believed in, gave your heart and soul to, betrays you and your heart hurts so much that it can barely beat. A true darkness arrived that would shadow every second, every moment and every day in the coming years. My world as I knew it had just died and I didn't know how I was ever going to move on.

I jump back to the present as my daughter comes bounding into the house, slamming the front door.

Tears are falling from her face.

I look at her and my heart breaks. Why must love always be so hard?

"He hates me! He doesn't want to ever see me a-again," she stutters through the endless tears falling from her eyes.

I know from experience that there is nothing I can do, nothing I can say that will take away the pain she is feeling at this moment. "I know you won't believe this, but I was once a teenager. I know how you feel…more than you can ever imagine," I say to her as memories of a first love and heartache begin to flood my mind.

CHAPTER ONE

Thirty-six years earlier

1977 – Age 14

Moving Day, June 25th

I was up all night. There was no way that I could sleep; it was like Christmas Eve. We were finally getting our own house. Up until today, we had lived in an apartment above my grandparents, where I'd lived for as long as I could remember.

There were only six houses on the block we were moving to and my house was right in the middle. It was nothing fancy or special, but in a couple of days, it would be ours. It was gray with a nice picture window that I envisioned my mom decorating with her plants. A huge tree took up most of our postage-stamp-sized lawn. The backyard looked pretty small too, but our dogs Winnie, a Yorkie; Henri, a poodle; and Toto, a silky terrier, were gonna love having their own yard to run around in.

Liz arrived early, just as she promised, to help us move in. Liz was my best friend. We met three years earlier, right before we finished fifth grade. We were both a part of a community service project, making ornaments for a local nursing home. We became instant friends.

Now, we had just graduated middle school a week before, and it couldn't have come soon enough. It'd been a complete nightmare for both of us. Without her friendship, I don't know how I could have gotten through those tormenting last three years. We seemed to be singled out early on. Two shy, awkward young girls, with not much fashion sense, gave every bully in the school cause to choose us as their targets. It didn't matter when we finally got the gist of what clothes to wear, how to fix our hair, or what makeup to use, the nasty comments always continued. Now that was finally all behind us. In September, we would go to high school and hope for things to be better.

"Come upstairs, I want to show you my room," I anxiously told her.

My room wasn't huge, but it was larger than the one at my grandmother's. The walls had light brown paneling on them, and my ceiling was pink. I had a nice-size closet, and I couldn't wait until all my clothes were hanging in it.

"It looks really great! Maybe we can get most of it set up today, if we can find the boxes with your stuff in it," Liz suggested.

"I hope so. I can't wait to sleep in here tonight. Let's go find some more boxes."

When we walked down the stairs, I heard a knock at the front door and went to answer it. Standing in front of me was a woman and two children.

The woman was holding a chocolate cake with strawberries on top. "Welcome to the neighborhood," she said with a huge smile on her face. "My name is Sarah, and this is David and Michele. They live on the corner of your street. I live directly across the street from you," she continued as she handed me the cake she was holding.

The boy looked about my age, medium build, with dark brown, longish hair, and his sister was a little younger. She was really cute and had wavy, long brown hair.

"Hi," they both greeted me.

"Hi," I said back. "Thank you for the cake. Let me get my parents." I felt sort of awkward, not knowing what to say to them. I found my parents in the kitchen unpacking and told them about the woman at the door. I saw Liz coming in the back door with a box. "Where did you go?" I asked her. "A neighbor and some kids were just at the door welcoming us to the neighborhood. Look at the cake they gave us."

"Wow. Yeah, I was out looking for more boxes with your name on them to unpack."

After working on my room for a couple of hours, we decided it was time for a break. The house was in chaos with boxes everywhere, as we made our way downstairs.

"There's a bunch of kids playing on the street. Are those the ones you met?" Liz asked as she looked out the front window.

I walked over and saw a bunch of kids. "Yes, two of them are the ones I met earlier. "Let me grab a couple cans of soda and we can sit outside on my front steps." I headed to the refrigerator.

"Don't you goof off too long; there's a lot to be done around here," my mom called out as we were heading out the door.

"We won't," I called back.

We sat on the stoop and watched all the kids playing street hockey. The two I met earlier waved when they saw me. I waved back and smiled. A few minutes later, I saw another boy about my age, heading towards me. My every instinct was to put my head down.

"Hey! I'm Danny. My brother and sister said they met you earlier."

I glanced up and when I saw him up close, my heart skipped a beat, fluttering uncontrollably. I've never felt anything like this before. I didn't know what was happening to me, but looking into his blue eyes made me feel like instant melting butter. "Hi, I'm Cassidy—umm—yes, I met them earlier." I was instantly dumbfounded as to what more to say. "This is my friend, Liz."

"Hi Liz. Nice to meet you."

"It's nice to meet you too, Danny," Liz replied, giving me a *holy cow* look that he couldn't see.

A warm feeling came over me, as I took in his athletic build, clearly visible in his blue jeans and t-shirt. I found myself staring at him, mesmerized by his every move and the sound of his voice. I forced myself to look away for a moment. When I glanced back, he was staring at me.

"Well, I'd better get back to the game, but I will talk to you later, okay?"

"Sure. I should get back to unpacking anyway," I replied as Liz and I headed back into the house. "Did you see his eyes? I couldn't stop staring at him. I think I'm going to really love living on this street."

"I noticed," Liz teased as she laughed.

We went back upstairs to my room and returned to emptying more boxes. I found that I couldn't stop thinking about Danny. I wondered when I would get to see him again. We managed to finish unpacking and setting up my room before Liz had to leave. I had hoped she could stay later, so we could sit outside again.

Exhaustion finally came crashing down as I climbed into my bed, in my new room that I loved. I closed my eyes as thoughts of Danny filled my head and dreams took over.

~* * * *~

Everyone was playing outside the next day when I gathered the courage to go sit on the steps alone.

As soon as Danny saw me, he came right over and sat down. "Did you get all unpacked yesterday?"

"Yes, my room is all done, but there's a lot more to do in the rest of the house." A quivering feeling began to churn in my formerly calm stomach. Why when I saw him did I instantly feel different? Not that I had much experience with boys, most were pretty mean to me in middle school. I didn't understand what was happening to me but—I liked it. A good-looking boy actually knew I existed and wanted to talk to me.

"Can you stay outside for a while? I'm going to play hockey for a bit, but I would also like to hang out with you...if you're going to be around?" he asked.

"Sure, I'll be around." I couldn't believe he wanted to spend time with me. Am I dreaming? I sat there, mesmerized by Danny's every move. I didn't know if it was minutes or hours later when he came back to sit with me.

We spent the next couple of hours talking about everything.

He was 15 years old and would be going into tenth grade in September. He told me about his brothers and sisters. I'd only met two of them—he had two more. His parents owned a beverage center in town, and he worked there whenever he could.

I told him that I was an only child and that I had been living not far away, before I moved to this neighborhood. As far as school was concerned, I didn't share with him my middle school experiences. I was afraid he might see me differently.

He also told me he was on the school hockey team and went on Sundays to practice.

I wasn't surprised by this. I could already tell that he loved the sport by watching him play all day and the day before.

He then said he would like me to go to one of his practices sometime.

I was ecstatic that he invited me. Oh, wow. A boy had never invited me anywhere before. I felt nervous suddenly and decided to try to move the conversation to something else. I went into a story about how last month, I was in my cousin's wedding party and had to dance with a boy for the first time.

When I told him the boy's name, his face changed.

"What? What's wrong?" I asked, worried that maybe I said something wrong.

"You're not going to believe this, but Jerry is one of my best friends. He told me about you and how he had to dance with a girl," Danny said with a laugh.

"No way! His brother married my cousin." I felt instant relief and smiled. How strange is it that he heard about me before we even met? I believe in destiny. Maybe there was a reason why we were meeting.

"Wait until I tell him that I met you. He did say the wedding went good and the dancing wasn't as bad as he thought it was going to be."

"It wasn't as bad as I thought it was going to be either. He's a nice guy. It was just strange, dancing with someone I didn't even know."

He asked me if I had ever gone out with someone. I'd only been one date, one night and it was a disaster. A boy asked me out to the pizza parlor and we met there. What he failed to tell me was that our *date* was dutch treat and that I was supposed to pay for my own food. It all felt awkward and we truly had nothing to say to each other. After we ate, we went our separate ways and avoided each other in school the rest of the year.

Danny and I continued to talk until he told me that he needed to go work and asked me if I would be around later.

I told him I would and to ring the doorbell when he got back. I watched as he walked away and continued to watch until he walked in through his front door. When I could no longer see him, my mind began to ramble over our conversation. I loved the way talking to him made me feel. I felt special, because he thought I was interesting enough to talk to. Not like how other boys had treated me up until now. Like they thought, I wasn't bright enough or pretty enough to spend time with. I really hoped he would come back soon. I went back inside and helped my mom unpack.

When the doorbell finally rang a few hours later, I nearly fell over the boxes in the middle of the room, rushing to get the door. I opened it and invited Danny inside to meet my parents.

CHAPTER TWO

My parents were cool with Danny. They treated him like he was just another one of the kids in the neighborhood. For the next week, we saw each other every day. He came over in the mornings. I made him breakfast and then eventually, lunch. We spent so much time talking, yet I couldn't tell you about what. It was everything and nothing at the same time. We were learning about each other on a deeper level, even if we didn't realize it at the time.

I did know something in me had changed since the day I met him, and continued to change every day after. It's inevitable that changes occur when your soul finds its other half—at least that's what I believed. I felt like a different person around him. I found myself laughing more, smiling all the time, and counting the seconds until I saw him again. I think I was meant to meet him.

Then, on July 1st, things became a little complicated for us. I was sitting in my bedroom, listening to some of my 45 records, when I happened to look out my window. I spotted Danny's brother, David as he put something into our mailbox. From his rapid movements, I could tell he was trying to do it unnoticed. Unfortunately for him, I was a very observant teenager. Intrigued, I went downstairs, my brain going a thousand miles a minute. *What did he put in there?* I went outside, opened flap and pulled out a letter, which read:

> *Cassidy,*
> *Even though I said asking a girl out in a note is not right, this is the only way I can do this. I was wondering if you would like to go the movies tonight to see Rollercoaster at Green Acres. I'll call you between 4:00 and 7:00, so you can give me your answer.*
> *David*
> *P.S. Michele gave me your number.*

My heart stopped. Why? After all the time I'd been spending with Danny, and his brother asks me out? What was I going to do? I folded the note back up and sat on my front stoop. I had no idea how long I'd been sitting out there.

"Are you okay?" Danny asked, his hands jammed into the front pockets of his pants.

His voice startled me and I'm sure I looked flustered because I'd just been thinking about him. "Yeah, I'm okay, just thinking."

Danny didn't look convinced as he sat down on the stoop beside me. "What were you thinking about? You look kind of sad."

"I'm not sad, it's just—your brother left me a note." I handed Danny the note and waited while he read it.

After a while, he finally said, "Oh. Do you umm, want to go out with him?"

"No. I mean, it's not that I don't like him, I just—I don't know him very well."

"Well, maybe you could get to know him if you went on a date with him."

I gave him a look that held so much meaning. Did he really think I wanted to go on a date with his brother? Had I misread his signals this whole time?

When Danny's eyes met mine, he must have seen the doubt in my eyes. "I think I can fix this," he said thoughtfully.

Now, I knew he finally understood. "Fix it how? I don't want to hurt his feelings, but—"

"I have an idea. What was the name of your friend again? I know you told me Liz is away on vacation, but the other one who was at your house the other day?"

"You mean Leslie?" I stared at him as if he'd grown two heads. Why did he want to know about my friend?

"Right. Is she dating anyone right now?"

"No."

"Well, maybe I can convince David to take her out on a date. Do you think she'd be interested?"

"How on earth are you going to convince him to go out with one of my friends?"

"Leave it to me! I can talk him into it," he said convincingly with a hopeful gleam in his eyes.

There was no mistaking his intent…he wanted his brother's interest turned to someone else, away from me. This simple fact shot through my body with a trembling excitement and my mind came alive with the possible meaning of it. Yes! He cared about me, more than I had previously thought.

For a moment, I considered his suggestion. Would David know why we were setting him up with my friend instead? I didn't want to hurt him, but I couldn't pretend there was anything more between us than there really was. "I guess I could ask her," I told him, feeling slightly more optimistic.

"There you go! Problem solved."

His smile was contagious, causing my own to spread across my lips in return. I couldn't help it. There was something endearing about this boy. He had my heart from the moment we met. "You really think it will be that easy? Do you think he'll know I didn't want to go out with him?" I played with the hem of my shirt, my nerves getting the best of me.

Danny shrugged. "I can try to make it sound like Leslie is better than you, but...she's not." He glanced up and our eyes met for a fleeting second, before he looked down again.

My heart thrummed with the potential meaning of that look and his words.

"We'll go on a double date."

My stomach began to flutter excitedly. It felt like a million butterflies were swarming inside of me. *A double date!* This meant I was going to get to go with Danny, which was what I wanted all along. It seemed as if he wanted it too. "I'll go give her a call and see if she's free tomorrow night." I felt really awful now, right on top of the happiness that bubbled inside of me. David was really nice and I liked him, but I felt a connection with Danny that I just couldn't explain. My heart wanted Danny, and it seemed like he wanted me too.

Later on, after I talked to Leslie on the phone about it and got her okay, Danny came back and said everything was fine. Somehow, he managed to convince David to go out with Leslie.

I would've loved to be a fly on the wall during that conversation. I had my doubts it would work, but I was overjoyed about it. I felt so anxious and nervous at the same time about our first date. I wanted everything to be perfect. I spent hours that afternoon, trying to figure out what I was going to wear and even put on a little bit of makeup. I tried to eat before leaving, but just couldn't.

Leslie arrived early, so we could finish getting ready. We anxiously waited for the boys to pick us up. When they showed up, I didn't know which one of us was more worried about the evening ahead. We walked to the bus stop— it wasn't too far—and there was total silence on the walk. Leslie and David didn't seem to be hitting it off exactly like we'd hoped, at least at that point. I hoped that it would get better as the night wore on.

All I kept thinking was what I was going to do if Danny tried to hold my hand. Did I want him to? Also, after my first dating experience, I wasn't sure if I was expected to pay for anything. So, I was preoccupied with that thought and I kept wondering if he liked the way I looked. Plus, a bunch of other stupid fears that was probably natural for a girl my age going on her first date. I kept hoping my palms wouldn't be sweaty if and when he took my hand. Or, that he wouldn't notice how anxious I was.

Danny and his brother were perfect gentleman and paid for all our tickets. During the bus ride, my heart kept beating fast, anticipating what might happen next. Would he try to hold my hand in the theatre, since it would be dark? Even though I had spent many days talking to him, being out on this *real* date was something I had never experienced before. The boys stopped to get us snacks at the concession stand. I felt guilty for wanting something but by now, of course, I was getting hungry. The smell of the fresh-popped popcorn was going to make my stomach start growling if I didn't get something.

As I reached to pull my wallet out, Danny asked me, "What would you like?"

I wanted everything by now but was afraid to order too much in case he was planning on paying. "I would like a small popcorn," I replied in almost a whisper, as I reached to pull out the $20 my mom had given me earlier. She knew what happened last time and made sure I was prepared.

"What are you doing?" Danny asked. "Put your money away, I got this."

"Are you sure?" I was in complete amazement here, thinking he must be really rich. It's strange having someone other than my parents buying something for me.

The theatre was crowded, but we found some empty seats in the back. Since there was that armrest that you have to share, we both avoided it. As the lights started to dim, my heart began to race again. He reached down to get his soda and his arm lightly touched my leg. Panic ran rampant through my thoughts. What if he tried to hold my hand soon? Should I keep it up on the armrest, so he could find it easily? It was so hard to concentrate on the movie because I was more worried about whether or not he would touch me. When the movie ended, I realized how we each seemed to stay in our own personal space. There was no handholding, but that was okay. I felt sure one day, he was going to and I hoped I would be ready by then.

There was less tension on the way back home and since we all enjoyed the movie, there was plenty of conversation about it. My first real date was a true success, a night I would always remember.

When we got back to my house, Danny walked me to the door. He didn't kiss me, just said that he would see me tomorrow. I went to my room, put on the radio, and laid on my bed. I wasn't tired at all. My mind was racing with too many thoughts of my evening. What was happening to me? Was it love at first sight? I kept seeing Danny's smile in my head. I couldn't wait for tomorrow to come.

CHAPTER THREE

Danny came over really early the next day. He decided he wanted to impress my dad, so while my parents were at work, he brought over his lawn mower. My dad hadn't had time to cut the grass since we moved in and had to go back to work. Danny's was only one of those push mowers, but it didn't matter. My dad was going to love him when he got home from work and saw that he wouldn't have to worry about the lawn.

I sat nearby and watched Danny's every move. He had shorts and a t-shirt on, nothing special, yet to me he was so good-looking, I couldn't take my eyes off him. I made him a cheeseburger for lunch and he took a break. We sat and ate together. In my mind, this was our second date, even though I knew that was a silly notion.

Shortly after he finished, he went home to take a shower and said he would be back later.

I started to pace, waiting for my dad to get home from work. As soon as I saw his car pull up, I went bursting outside. I couldn't wait for him to see how Danny did the lawn for him. I was so proud of him and I was sure my dad would share in the excitement.

"Who touched the lawn?" my father asked me, and not with the happy voice that I was expecting.

"Danny!" I replied way too cheerfully. "He wanted to surprise you. The grass was so high and he knew you wouldn't have time, so he brought over his mower." I then waited for my dad to be as overjoyed as I was.

One look at my dad's face as he went to see the backyard told me he didn't share in my joy. I had no idea what the problem could be. I knew my dad had a major obsessive-compulsive disorder, which I had been dealing with all my life. My dad had to have perfection. It was a very high standard to live with.

"Well, don't you think if you are going to mow the lawn, you should have scooped up all the dog crap from the yard first?" he asked in a stern tone.

I knew that tone all too well. This wasn't what I was hoping for. "Oh," was the only word I could say, as my bubbles of happiness faded away.

I then became afraid my dad was going to be nasty to Danny, but when Danny showed up later that night, my dad didn't say a word to him about the lawn mowing. He thanked him politely and never said another word about it to him. Somehow, though I knew I would hear about it for a long time.

~* * * *~

The morning of July 7th began like any other. I made Danny scrambled eggs…for some strange reason he loved my eggs. We went outside and sat on the front stoop, when out of nowhere he said, "Will you go out with me?"

"What?" I replied, making him repeat it, so I could hear the words again. In my head, I was jumping up and down and screaming. My face must have looked like a Christmas tree all lit up. "Yes," I answered as soon as my shock wore off and my smile was small enough to speak. I didn't want him to leave, yet I wanted to call all my girlfriends to tell them. I had a boyfriend, and even that day's date was special…magical, it was 7/7/77.

I loved having a boyfriend. I also loved that there was no school and I could see him every day and every night. We spent endless hours talking together. There was a ninety-nine cents movie theatre in town. Since it was cheap, we could go again and again, to see the same movie. At the rate we were going, we would have seen *Annie Hall* twenty times by the end of the summer. Every morning, he came over and I cooked him breakfast. He said that my scrambled eggs were 'legendary,' as were my cheeseburgers.

I didn't know if it was my idea or his, but one night we decided to write questions to each other. He asked me the following questions:

Question 1 – Do you want to get married? Y or N

Question 2 – How many kids do you want? 1, 2, 3, 4

Question 3 – Are we going to hold hands when we walk to high school? Y or N

Question 4 – Do you want to kiss? Y or N

Question 5 – Will we ever make out? Y or N

I loved this! I could also ask him questions and not be embarrassed. I could ask him anything I wanted to, without having to say it out loud or see his face directly.

Back then, we didn't have computers, text messaging, or any of the technology that we do today. We would communicate all the time by paper, leaving letters in each other's mailboxes. When one of us needed the other to know that there was a letter, we would ring the phone once. Think of it as the ding on your cell phone, telling you that you have a text message. This could have been the early stages of texting. Calling each other and communicating face to face didn't come easy for us. Being young and in our first relationship, we were both extremely shy.

One day, I was sitting in my room listening to my 45's and albums. I really loved listening to my music. I'd just gotten a new record the day before and kept playing it over and over. I turned the volume up, and the bass from *Wouldn't It Be Nice,* by the Beach Boys began to shake my room. I was startled when Danny came walking in.

"I want you to come over and meet my mom and dad today," he announced.

I suddenly realized, he'd been at my house every day, so he had met my parents a long time ago. "Sure," I said, but inside I wasn't looking forward to it. What if his parents didn't like me?

I followed him to his house. It was so nice that he lived so close.

Danny walked into the house first and headed to the kitchen.

I walked slowly behind him, dreading this moment.

"Mom, Dad," Danny called quite loudly.

"What?" Danny's dad called back.

I heard his footsteps getting closer and glanced up.

There stood his dad in his underwear. "Umm, Daniel, do you think you could have told me that we had company?" His dad's voice sounded stern as he quickly retreated back from where he had come.

"I told you I was bringing Cassidy over today," Danny said, his voice now quivering.

If his dad was a cartoon character, I imagine steam would've been blowing out of his ears right about then.

I didn't know what to do or say, so I just looked around the room and tried to find something to stare at.

His dad came back out with clothes on.

Danny's mom was right behind him, laughing hysterically at what had just transpired.

"Hi, Cassidy, sorry about that," he said in a jolly voice that reminded me of Santa Claus.

"That's okay," was the cleverest thing I could think of to say. What do you say to someone you just met for the first time and they only had underwear on?

His mom and dad made small talk. His dad told me that they owned Lynbrook Cold Beer & Beverage. Danny and his brothers all worked at their business.

I had walked past it so many times but now, I knew that my boyfriend's family owned it. *My boyfriend*—that still sounded funny to me.

Danny and I left shortly after. It was hard to get past the awkwardness of the moment, but somehow we managed to. I got the feeling we would talk about this incident a lot in the days to come.

Later that night, I got to meet Danny's older brother Raymond, and he asked us if we wanted to go take a ride to Jack in the Box for some tacos. The boys told me that they were the best. His brother was the tallest of the three boys. He also had the same somewhat long, dark brown hair. Raymond popped in an eight-track of the Raspberries and off we went.

When we pulled into Jack in the Box, Danny asked me what I wanted.

I was still having a hard time with him paying for everything. Even though the food there smelled so good and I really did want a taco, the words, "nothing, thanks" came out of my mouth. I had to get past this or I was going to have a lot of hungry days and nights.

Then, on the ride home, we saw a falling star. "What did you wish for?" I asked, dying to know if his wish included me.

"I can't tell you."

"Why not?"

"You don't tell wishes. If you do, then they don't come true."

Maybe he wished for someone else? To have another girlfriend? So many negative thoughts were going through my mind. None of them made sense but to me that didn't matter at the time. The rest of the car ride home, I didn't say a word to him. I was furious by then. I wanted to know that wish. As soon as we got back to his house, I left.

I couldn't explain why knowing the wish was so important to me, but it was. Maybe I was wrong, but considering that he was my first boyfriend, I thought we would be sharing everything, even wishes on stars. I felt crushed. I quickly sat down, got out pen and paper, and wrote him a letter. All I could think was that if he didn't want to share his wish, then it couldn't be something good. I folded up the letter, ran to the corner of my street and across the way. I put it in his mailbox, ran home, and rang his phone once. I sat waiting patiently for his response. It seemed like hours but it was only minutes before my phone rang once. I nearly fell down the stairs racing to get my note back with his response. I quickly opened it and found the words:

"I can't tell you what I wished for. I already told you if I do, then it won't come true. I am sorry, if you want to break up over this, there is nothing I can do."

Break up? I didn't want to break up over this. I would get it out of him one day. I had to know what it was. For now, I needed to get over this, or I was going to lose him.

I never did find out what he wished for that night. It was our first big fight and I will always remember it. How silly it seems to me now that I would make a mountain out of something so simple. At the time, it felt like the end of the world to not know what that wish was about. At fourteen, the simplest things seemed to be such huge dilemmas when they truly weren't.

~* * * *~

Danny and I went to town one day to walk around. While strolling, he extended out his hand to me.

He wants to hold my hand?

He then proceeded to ask me for a piece of gum.

I couldn't say anything to him about it at the time, but I was devastated. I couldn't believe I actually wanted him to hold my hand. I promised myself that that night, I would talk to him about it. I wrote:

Question – Did you know that I thought that you wanted to hold my hand today?

His response to me was, *"No."*

Just a simple no was his only response. He didn't even think about holding my hand.

Then I became preoccupied with the fact that I had never kissed a boy before, so I hoped maybe this was truly becoming a summer of firsts. I had my first date, then a first boyfriend. I was so scared of my first kiss, yet I was constantly wondering when he was going to try to kiss me.

One night, while hanging out with the neighborhood kids, we were dared during truth or dare. We were told to go behind the wall at the end of my street and kiss. I think my heart nearly stopped right there.

"Don't worry," Danny said. "It will be really fast." He probably knew I was upset about kissing for the first time.

If I didn't let him kiss me, everyone would laugh at me and I would be back in middle school once again. I was so sick of being tormented by the other kids. *You are going into high school in September. You can't do something that will give anyone a reason to make fun of you.* This was my chance to start anew. I wish I would've told him about my fears of being the object of more ridicule. "Okay," I replied. "As long as it's really fast."

We went behind the wall, so no one could see us. I couldn't believe this was happening to me. I thought that I'd finally convinced myself that I could actually do this as I leaned on the wall. I knew it was coming and seconds seemed like minutes. Did I really want this to happen? What am I supposed to do? As he leaned into kiss me, panic set in and I quickly moved away. Luckily, he didn't bang his face on the wall, but it was close. All I could think of was that I would be laughed at for sure over this.

"Don't worry. I'll tell them we did," Danny said, his words sounding magical to me. He took my hand as we made our way out from behind the wall.

We were holding hands! I was up in the clouds, I was flying, I felt so happy. I trusted that he wouldn't tell anyone that I chickened out.

The next night, we were playing truth or dare again. Since I moved there, I noticed the neighborhood kids all loved doing this every night. Danny took my hand again, that night. I was ecstatic and suddenly felt so safe. All of a sudden, I heard those words again.

"I dare you to kiss Danny," Michelle teased. The tone of her voice told me she knew we didn't kiss the night before.

He wouldn't have told his siblings, would he? It was dumb of me to think that this wouldn't happen again, after last night.

As soon as we got behind the wall, I asked him with a bit of an angry tone, "You didn't tell your sister that we didn't kiss, did you?

"No, of course not. I understand why we didn't," he responded in a voice that somehow told me he wasn't lying.

"Really?" I instantly felt relief. "We won't have to lie tonight," I stated with a sudden flare of courage. In my mind, I knew we couldn't put this off forever.

I leaned back against the same wall that saw me flee from kissing him the night before, the same wall that almost broke his nose. He came towards me and we finally kissed. I felt really awkward, strange and yet, I saw fireworks all at once. I could only imagine that my face was bright red. We went out from behind the wall still holding hands. He held my hand the rest of the night and I was in pure heaven. That night I wrote in my diary:

August 16, 1977
Dear Diary:
Tonight we kissed for the first time. We were playing truth or dare again and his sister dared us. I couldn't chicken out on him again, after last night. It wasn't as bad as I thought it was going to be, it was fun! Write again tomorrow!

'It was fun' was the only creative phrase my 14-year-old brain could come up with to describe the first kiss I ever had. Even after we shared our first kiss, kissing wasn't something that came naturally to us. We even got creative enough to plan them. One time, he was to go up the stairs, I was to come down them, and we would meet in the middle to kiss. We met in the middle as planned and wound up not even kissing.

Life was simple back then. We sat with my piles of 45s and albums and picked our songs. We decided on, *I Just Want to be Your Everything* by Andy Gibb as our together song, *When I Need You* by Leo Sayer was his song to me, and *Higher and Higher* by Rita Coolidge was my song to him. Simple, yet life was good.

During that summer, we also babysat a little girl around the corner from us. She was the cutest thing, only two and that's such a fun age. Her name was Christy. She would come to my house all the time for breakfast. She loved to be with us and it made us feel like a married couple. We would take her up to town, imagining that she was ours and we were a family. We went to Woolworths and bought matching friendship rings that looked like wedding rings. We wore them every day. We even talked about getting a pre-engagement ring for our one-year anniversary.

On a summer night while he was babysitting Christy, I wasn't supposed to be there. We had gotten the hang of 'making out' by now. All of a sudden, we heard Christy's parents. They came home earlier than they were supposed to. It was a good thing I was able to run fast and leap the fence right into my own backyard in a matter of seconds. We didn't get caught, but it was really close.

Even though we were getting used to making out with each other, we weren't prepared to witness it happening with other people in a movie—and while sitting next to my parents. For some unknown reason, my parents decided to take us to see *The Other Side of Midnight,* an R-rated movie. The sex scenes and naked people in that movie were not for young eyes. They were doing things we weren't even writing about in questions yet. I still don't know why my parents took us to it, and unfortunately, I couldn't even ask them why. I couldn't tell you a single thing about this movie, other than it was very inappropriate for teens to see.

During that summer, I realized how everyone seemed to be friends in our neighborhood and I loved it. Danny told me about a huge block party that was planned. He thought it might be a good time to invite my parents, so that they could meet his parents. Danny even gave me a t-shirt for the occasion. *Cherry Lane Gang* was written across the front. I couldn't wait to wear it!

The day of the block party finally arrived. We spent all day setting up the tables and chairs. I finally felt like I fit in, and my dread of going to high school had been replaced with a sense of tentative anticipation.

In my wildest dreams, I never thought that Danny's parents and mine would hit it off so fast. Danny and I watched them sitting together, laughing and talking the whole night, when we weren't behind the dead-end wall kissing. We even heard that they made plans to get together the next weekend.

When the party was over, I asked Danny to take a walk with me. I had to go to my old street to take care of my friend's dog. I had promised her before I moved that I would help her out. I figured it would be easy and they were going to give me some money. They had an Old English Sheep Dog; his name was Running Meat. The name suited him—he was huge. He had long straggly hair that covered his eyes and everywhere else.

When we got there, I opened the door to let him out, then Danny and I sat on her steps, waiting for the dog to finish his business. We both noticed that he seemed to be having a hard time with things. What should have been a quick walk was taking much longer. He finally started walking towards us but was walking funny.

I went behind him and saw what the problem was. There hanging on his behind was his poop. I didn't know what to do. I couldn't let him go back in the house covered in crap. He would get it all over the carpeting. But my friend was trusting me to take care of her dog. I immediately came up with a plan. "I need you to clean his butt for me," I said to Danny with the sweetest voice I could muster.

"You can't be serious?" he replied with a look of pure horror. "I am not going near that thing."

"If you don't then I will break up with you." I needed to clean up this dog and I knew there was no way I was going to do it.

Danny stood there thinking about what I just said to him.

I couldn't believe those words had actually came out of my mouth. I didn't want to break up, but I felt desperate now.

Danny didn't say a word, just got up and walked over to the hose. "You hold him and I will spray him with the hose."

I didn't care what he did as long as I didn't have to deal with it. It took a while to get him all clean, but we did and I put him back in the house.

The walk home was spent in gloomy silence. Why did I say those words? I think I just tested his love for me and he passed.

Danny acted very strange the days following the block party. I eventually realized that he was a moody person, which was hard to deal with at times. Maybe he was thinking about the other night when I threatened to break up with him. His moods and my PMS seemed to put a strain on us. He didn't understand what I would go through every month and I didn't understand why he got so cranky for no reason. He could be in a good mood one minute, and then be in the worst mood the next. One day, he threw one of my special stuffed animals on the floor and I told him to leave. I didn't want to see him *ever* again. He was halfway down the street when I found myself calling him back and apologizing. We would often break up over silly, stupid things like that, and then get right back together.

"I love you, always and forever," Danny said to me one day for the first time to my face.

"I love you too, forever and always," I said back. It felt strange saying this, even though it was how I felt.

"Not forever and always," he countered with a smile. "It's always and forever."

"No. It's forever and always. You know I like to be different." I laughed.

I loved him and he loved me. I couldn't wait to hear him say the words to me again.

The night before school started, I heard the phone ring once and knew that there was a letter in my mailbox. I was excited, but wondered why he wrote me a letter. I was also afraid to go see what it said, since he'd been acting cranky recently. I wasn't at all prepared for the letter I was about to read.

Cassidy,
See it is like this, if I walk to school with you tomorrow, it is going to put a bad impression on your friends and mine. They'll

think you have me to do anything you want me to do. It is not that I don't love you, that is not true, and if we hang around each other all the time, we both won't have any friends. I have already lost two good friends because all we did was be together, but I loved it very much. I am just trying to say if all we do is hang around each other, we will have no friends. What if we ever broke up? You don't have to agree.

I love you, Danny

WHAT? Was he serious? He didn't want to walk to school with me? He lost friends because of me?

I quickly wrote back to him: *"What two friends did you lose?"* I ran to his mailbox, put it inside, ran home, and rang his phone once.

I heard my phone ring and ran back to the mailbox.

He wrote: *"It doesn't matter. If we walk to school everyone from north and south will think that you have me wrapped around your finger."*

I was getting really mad by then. As I wrote him back, my handwriting was starting to look more like scribble: *"Well, if that is true that you lost your friends because of me, I guess we should just break up."* I ran to his mailbox, ran home, and rang his phone once.

I heard my phone and this time, my parents yelled to me, "Will you two stop with the phone!"

Now what do I do? I quickly read his latest response. *"Meet me outside. I have some bad news to tell you and I don't want to break up."*

I ran outside. "What is the bad news?" I asked, my voice trembling.

"I can't play hockey this year," he told me in a voice like he felt his life was over.

I'd been watching him play hockey on our dead-end street most of the summer with his brothers and his best friend, Bobby. He was really good at it. I knew that he was planning on trying out for the school team. "Why can't you play?"

"The coach told me since my grades were not high enough and I cut class too many times last year, I'm not allowed to even try out."

There were no words to say back. I was just happy that we weren't broken up. I didn't even bring up the walking to school part again. We decided that we were going to try to cut down on our phone ringing because our parents were getting really annoyed by it. Danny then told me he would throw tiny rocks at my window.

When I heard something hitting my window the next night, it didn't sound like rocks. It sounded like a loud splatting. It was dark out, so I couldn't see anything. I went downstairs and heard Danny whistling. "What did you throw at my window?" I asked him.

"I couldn't find a rock, so I grabbed a couple of tomatoes from your neighbor," he explained with a laugh.

"Oh, no!" I exclaimed. "You know how my dad is. When he sees tomatoes on the roof he is going to flip." I was pretty freaked out. I hoped my dad wouldn't notice, but who was I kidding?

The next morning when my OCD dad saw the roof, freaking out would have been better than the wrath that I heard. I couldn't help but laugh a bit when he spent hours cleaning it and getting every bit of tomato off the roof. Danny certainly was going to be on the shit list, so to speak.

Even though I knew my dad was really mad, he jokingly said to Danny that the next time he wanted to see me, to please just come to the door or go back to the phone ringing. It would be better than having to clean up tomatoes again.

The days all seemed to blend together and before I knew it, it was Christmas time. I was so anxious for Christmas that year. It was going to be our first year in our house and I couldn't wait to decorate. I was also incredibly happy to have a boyfriend to share the holidays with. He even helped decorate the tree with us.

My mother was really great at knitting, and had knitted Danny an awesome sweater that I couldn't wait for him to see. I got him a nice ID bracelet.

On Christmas day, he handed me a box. I wanted it to be jewelry. When I opened the box I found a beautiful heart necklace, and engraved on the back was, "Love, Danny." In the card he had written, *"You will have to wait for your other gift. It is an ankle bracelet."* I was completely and utterly on top of the world at that very moment. I knew I was going to marry this boy someday. I could feel it in every ounce of my soul. I immediately put the necklace on. I couldn't wait for everyone to see it and see how much he loved me.

A week later, he handed me an ankle bracelet. It was perfect and beautiful to me, with two hearts. Someday, maybe we would add our initials on the hearts, but that would mean I would have to part with it to have it done. I didn't ever want to take it off.

We never did walk to school together, even though I knew him throughout all my high school years and we lived only houses away from each other. I often wondered what magnetic power he possessed over me. Why would I put up with so much and still keep going back for more. My only excuse was love, pure, innocent, and simple. I loved him. I never shared so much of my soul with any other person ever in my life.

CHAPTER FOUR

1978 – Age 15

It was the first day of the New Year. My parents took Danny and me out to dinner. I really loved that my parents were okay with him being around all the time. The restaurant was really crowded. I glanced over at Danny, who was in the middle of a conversation with my dad and they were both laughing. That was what I wanted more than anything. It was so nice to see them talking and laughing. I gazed out the window and saw the snow starting to come down really hard. I noticed just how much more beautiful snow looks when you're in love. That's crazy, right? It just billows down in such a calm way and everything is covered in a white wonderland.

Dinner went by quickly; in a way, it went by too fast. I loved being with my family and Danny. It made me think of what our lives together would be like when we got older, having nice holiday meals with my parents.

We got into the car for the short drive home. When we pulled up to my house, I saw that everyone was on my street playing in the snow. Danny walked off and started talking to his brother. I thought he would come back to where I was, but he didn't. I felt really left out.

We'd just had a great day and now for some reason, he was acting like he was mad at me. Every so often, he came near me, but then he just knocked me into the snow.

I tried to laugh it off. It was funny but I wasn't happy that he kept ignoring me. I pulled him aside and asked him what was wrong. He told me we were probably going to break up and it was just a feeling. I knew it must have been more than that. Did I miss something? It seemed every week there was something. I didn't understand how someone could be so happy one minute and then change into someone I didn't know the next. I'd never met someone who was as moody as Danny.

Our six-month anniversary arrived and of course, we had another fight over something dumb. I didn't even know how it started or why. When he left that night, my mother told me she might forbid me from seeing him. She was tired of all the fighting...I was too. I ran to my room and cried until I had no more tears to shed. I didn't want to lose him but I didn't know why

all we did was fight. I kept asking myself why I
loved someone who was always so difficult.
After my tears had run dry, I got up, got a piece
of paper, and wrote down my feelings. It was
my first poem.

A love so deep down
Your heart beats so fast
I could never think of life
If you were my past
I've learned all about you
It seems only a short time
I feel in my heart
That you are really mine
I need your love and support
For the rest of my life
My only dream
Is to one day be your wife
The love we have
Is so very strong
Which only means
Together is where we belong

Then there was the ring of my phone, a note
in the mailbox, and all was right in the world yet
again.
We were both working at making our
relationship better. For the time being, the
fighting had calmed down. We were
handholding and making out all the time, yet we
still had a shyness between us. A conversation

about taking our relationship to the next level and making love would lead to a set of questions that would change everything for me and a plan would be set into motion.

Question 1 – Did you honestly ever do it?
No.
Question 2 – Are you sure you get a 'you know what'?
Yes.
Question 3 – Are you serious?
Yes.
Question 4 – Do you love me enough?
Yes.
Question 5 – Are we going to keep breaking up and having stupid fights?
Hopefully not.
Question 6 – Do you want me to try and get on the pill?
If you want.
Question 7 – What if somehow I got pregnant, which I absolutely better not.
You won't.

This was not a spur of the moment decision, but something that was discussed for weeks and planned out completely. The night was set for a Saturday when my parents would be out.

The day arrived and that night, our plan would be carried out. The monsters living in my stomach were in full force. It was hard to look into my parents' eyes, knowing what I was going to do. Not long after they were out of the house, I would become a woman and be a different person. I believed this with every ounce of my soul. As soon as they closed the door, I rang his phone once—the signal that they were gone and it was time to come over. Even though it took only seconds for him to walk to my house, it seemed like forever. He walked into my living room and our eyes met. It was time; that night we were taking our love to the next step. It was so hard to look at him knowing what we were going to do.

"When do you want to go upstairs?" His voice was a whisper I could barely hear.

My heart stopped dead, so many thoughts running around in my brain. I felt so scared. "Did you bring it with you?" I quickly asked. If he didn't, then I was off the hook.

"Yes," he mumbled.

"Why don't we watch a movie first?" Clearly, I was stalling.

"Okay," he said, in a voice that sounded relieved.

I didn't watch the movie. Well, my eyes stared at the television but my mind was not with me. It was thinking of what was going to happen when the movie was over.

The movie ended too soon and it was time. I didn't want to wait too long and risk my parents coming home.

My hands were all sweaty. Maybe it was my outfit choice—a sweat suit, which was bright yellow. I probably glowed in the dark, which would not have been good. My heart began to race. I knew it was now or never, at least if we were to do it tonight.

He reached out to me.

I took his hand and we went up the stairs. We kept the lights off. It was easier to not have to look at each other in the face. I knew mine must have looked like my sweaty palms had met with a light socket.

We sat on the edge of my bed and time stood still. We finally started making out with a faster pace than we had before. Maybe if we sped up, this would be over and I would soon be safely back in my living room.

I put my mind outside my body and didn't let myself think about what was happening. I closed my eyes really tight and when I opened them, we were sitting once again on the edge of my bed and it was over. Was I dreaming? That was what everyone talked about? I was a woman now? I didn't feel different. It was so quick. Is that the way it always is?

I couldn't see his face. Was he happy? Did I do what I was supposed to?

"I'll meet you downstairs." His words broke into my thoughts.

"Okay, I'll be right down," I responded. Was my voice still the same now that I was a woman?

I walked into the bathroom and looked in the mirror. I didn't look different. Shouldn't I? It was so intimate. I should have felt happy about sharing my body and soul with him, yet I was embarrassed. Maybe I did something wrong or didn't meet his expectations. I was surprised that it didn't hurt like I thought it was going to. Part of me wanted to just stay in the bathroom, but I didn't want to take too long. He would wonder what I was doing. I finally mustered up some courage and made my way back downstairs.

When I walked into the living room, our eyes didn't make contact. There was an awkwardness between us now. I didn't think *doing it* was what he envisioned either. Maybe he thought we weren't meant to be together.

I hurriedly put the television back on. *"Butterflies are Free* is coming on," I said. "Let's watch that." I didn't even care what was on the screen as long as something broke the silence.

I didn't foresee us planning another encounter anytime soon and relief took over. I didn't want to disappoint him again. I believed I was the reason it wasn't the magical encounter it was supposed to have been. This was supposed to be a night I would remember the rest of my life. I definitely would, but not in the way, it should have been remembered. The rest of the evening was spent watching television and avoiding eye contact.

I walked him to the door when it was time for him to leave. I wasn't sure if we would even speak.

He took me in his arms and hugged me. Our eyes finally met.

"I love you, always and forever," he whispered as our eyes locked.

"I love you, too, forever and always," I said right back.

"There you go again, always and forever." He laughed as he walked out the door and faded into the night.

I felt so glad he said that to me when he left. After our less than perfect night, I wasn't sure he still felt the same way about me.

We didn't talk about that night for a very long time. We shared another first with each other that night, yet it wasn't exactly the dreamy night we both thought it was going to be. It also didn't change how our relationship path would go. We didn't fight any less than before and as much as we seemed to want to be together, fate always had something else in store.

I loved that my mother loved him like a son. I worried about whether his being over every day would upset my parents, but they seemed to be fine with it. One day, he added chocolate pudding to my mother's shopping list. She laughed about it to me, but went and bought it for him. To my mother, who always wished that I wasn't an only child, this was the son she dreamed of having.

Time moved swiftly and before I know it, it was spring.

My dad took the day off work one day and said he was going to paint the garage. Danny and I said we would help him. The look on his face told me that he wasn't all that happy with our offer. I wondered why. I guessed he was still thinking about the lawn mowing incident.

"You two can paint the back of the garage," my dad instructed in a voice that meant, 'no way do I trust you two with anything that can be seen.' He handed us two paintbrushes and a can of gray paint.

"Okay," I said to him. I got to spend the day with Danny and I thought painting would be fun. I went upstairs and put on an old Mickey Mouse t-shirt in case any paint got on me. I didn't want to be wearing a shirt that I cared about.

I was happy we were doing the back of the garage. That way, my dad couldn't see us and watch over everything we did. My dad was very critical, so I wanted it to be perfect, or as perfect as we could make it. Danny and I started off really well. We were both being really careful and neat. That was until a giant plop of paint fell onto the ground, which caused us to laugh. It was just the funniest thing to us. A bad case of those giggles that you can't stop took us over. He took the paintbrush and ran it down the back of my shirt.

"Now, you are going to get it," I threatened, my laughter uncontrollable. I peeked around the back of the garage. I didn't see my dad in sight for the moment. I took my brush and painted his shirt. Now it was war. He painted me and I painted him. In a matter of minutes, we were both covered in paint.

My stomach was killing me from laughing. Tears were running down my face. In my mind, I was thinking 'my dad is going to kill us.'

"How are you two doing back there?" my dad's voice broke our laughter for a second.

"Umm, we're good, Dad," I replied as laughter still had control of me and I couldn't stop. I knew I needed to stop laughing but I just couldn't. A plop of paint fell from my head and it started all over again.

"Are you two kidding me?" my father said as he rounded the garage and Danny and I came into view. His voice showed that he clearly was not happy, but he also had to smile at the sight of us. "Drop the brushes, get the hose, and spray some of that off!"

I stared at his face, hoping for a smile. I didn't see any signs of him thinking it was funny. I grabbed the hose and started to spray off the paint. When I finished, I was completely soaked and still covered in paint, Danny took the hose and did the same. The laughter began again. I was trying to think of something, anything to keep from laughing.

"Get out of here now, so I can clean this up!" My dad's voice boomed over the laughter that was again, out of control.

I was bent over from pain. I couldn't see anymore with the tears pouring and my eyes burning.

My mother went to the door to see what was going on. A smile spread across her face. She disappeared for a moment, and reappeared with towels in her hands. She opened the door and handed the towels to us.

We grabbed them and ran up my driveway to the front of my house—as far away from my dad's anger as we could get. We sat on my stoop and the laughter took over again.

"I bet my dad thinks we're drunk or something," I said in a breathless voice.

"I'm going to go home and change," Danny managed to get out. "I think you should come to my house when you're changed. I don't think we should hang out here for a while."

That night, my dad didn't say a word about our fiasco, which was a good thing.

I vowed I would never ask to paint again. Danny didn't want to come over, unless my dad wasn't home for a couple days following that incident.

When my dad and Danny did come face to face again, the garage incident wasn't mentioned.

We liked to go to the movies a lot, and even though Leslie and David didn't hit it off, they had become good friends and went out with Danny and me on the weekends. We went to the movies, or bowling. I was really happy that they were able to find a way to get along.

Then hanging out and fooling around at Danny's house turned disastrous one night. His brother was smoking in the house. Somehow, a lit ash fell onto a pillow. All of a sudden, we all smelled something burning.

"Do something with it!" Danny yelled.

"I think it's finally out," his brother replied.

"I think mom and dad are going to notice the burn mark, better throw the pillow out. Bury it in the pail outside."

"Maybe they won't notice," his brother responded in a frenzied voice.

I'm not sure who came up with the idea. I knew my parents would instantly notice a pillow missing from our couch. I couldn't imagine how his parents wouldn't notice. Perhaps that was because I was an only child. Maybe if I had four brothers and sisters, my parents wouldn't notice things as much.

It wasn't long after these words were spoken that we heard a car pull up.

"Just act natural," everyone said.

A very loud and very angry voice shortly followed. "Get out here! The garbage pail is on fire!" His dad's enraged voice filled the air.

We all ran in different directions away from the fire and Danny's dad.

A quick glance at the side of the house revealed flames like I'd never seen before. They were really high, coming out of the garbage pail. By now, all the contents of the pail were also on fire.

"I think I better get home," I softly whispered to Danny. "Good luck!" I didn't want to be in the path of whatever was heading their way. It would be days before we could all hang out again.

The school year ended and summer was upon us. We were anxious to be able to hang out and not have to worry about school for a couple of months. One would think our carelessness in the past would keep us on our toes, but we were teenagers. It was summer after all, and all we were thinking about was having fun.

Earlier in the week, Danny's mom had gone out and purchased some really nice lawn chairs. She, too, was looking forward to the summertime weather. But one night of truth or dare, a large group of teenagers and her beautiful new lawn chairs met their fate behind the famous *dead-end wall.* " The chairs were never to be seen again. It happened initially and purely by accident. A whole bunch of people sat on them, causing one to collapse. It shouldn't have been funny, but it was. Of course, the other had to be tested, to see how many it could hold. Before we knew it, they weren't looking like chairs anymore, but collapsed messes. So, they needed to be hidden.

Later on, Danny's mom questioned us all about them, and couldn't understand how they all could just disappear. Not one of us ever gave up what happened to them.

One day, we went to a place called Nunley's. It was a small amusement park with carousel horses, a rollercoaster, games, and miniature golf. We found a machine where you could make your own good luck charms. Danny and I made up charms with our names and our special date, 7/7/77, on them. I thought about how nice it would be when Danny got his license and we could go there by ourselves.

On Sundays, we went to Racket and Rink with Danny's family. He was on an ice hockey team and they were practicing for the new season. I loved going and watching him play. We would all pile into his mom's station wagon. I was so happy that they let me go also. Danny's mom would quickly turn on WHN, a radio station that played country music. She probably felt that anything was better than listening to a car full of teenagers. My parents also only listened to that station, so I was used to hearing the songs. One Sunday, we were cruising along when the song *Mommas, Don't Let Your Babies Grow Up to be Cowboys* filled the car. We all started singing along and laughing to it.

When Danny was playing icy hockey, I knew he was truly happy. He loved to skate and he was really good at it.

One day, when Danny went to my house for breakfast, I made him my legendary scrambled eggs. That's what he called them, anyway. I don't know what made them so good, but he loved them. By accident, ketchup got on the white pants I was wearing. And I had never really used the washing machine. Guess it might have been smart to pay attention to what my mom did. I didn't want her to see my pants ruined, so Danny and I decided that we could wash them.

We figured out how to start the machine and put in soap. Moments later, it was working. We went back upstairs and watched television to pass the time.

"I am going to go check on the pants," I told him.

He sat there mesmerized by the television.

I knew he would probably fall asleep if I was gone too long. My mother would say all the time, "That boy could fall asleep on a picket fence." He was always falling asleep. One minute he seemed wide awake and the next he was out cold.

Anyway, I walked down the stairs and as I turned the corner towards the washing machine, I saw bubbles—lots and lots of bubbles. The bubbles were coming out of the top of the machine. "Danny!" I shouted as loud as I possibly could. "Come here quick! Oh my god, what have I done now?"

"What?" he called out.

I could hear his footsteps getting closer.

"Holy shit, what did you do?"

"I don't know. I guess I put too much soap," I responded, thinking what a dumb question that was to ask me now. "Get something, we have to get rid of these bubbles." I was flipping out by that time.

He went back upstairs and returned to me with two Dixie cups from the kitchen. "It's all I could find," he replied to me as his laughter began.

We bailed bubbles for at least an hour, with just two little Dixie cups, and laughed so hard our stomachs hurt. I grabbed the mop and cleaned everything up, so there was no trace of our mishap. The rest of the day, every time we looked at each other all we did was laugh. No one ever knew why, but we did.

Danny and I continued to have great days, and then again, we would break up over something purely stupid. But in a short time we once again, would be back together. No matter how mad we each seemed to get, our fights never did last very long. In many ways, he was the complete gentleman. Whenever we went somewhere, I was never allowed to pay, no matter what I was buying, and my girlfriends were not allowed to pay either.

School began once again. Summers always went by too fast. I didn't bring up walking to school, remembering the past. Days all seemed to blend together when we had to worry about school work and grades. The holidays crept up on us fast, too. We'd blink an eye and it was Halloween, then Thanksgiving, and before we knew it, we were putting up the Christmas tree again.

Danny continued to confuse me. Just when I thought that we were on the right path, something would happen and we would be back to square one. I made excuses for him—he was tired or he had a headache. I always found a reason to explain his behavior. I didn't want to even think about the possibility that his love for me wasn't like my love for him.

Our families gave up trying to figure out if we were together or not. No one could keep up. We were either together and happy or apart and miserable. At the time, these stupid things were mountains in our way. Try as we might to move those mountains, fate would take us a different way, apart.

CHAPTER FIVE

1979 – Age 16

Happiness didn't last long for me. By the time I was 16, Danny's moodiness would start a fight that ended in a break up that didn't end as quickly as the others did. I was now supposed to move on and not care. I didn't know how I was supposed to forget about him. I didn't want to. I missed having him with me and having someone to hang out with.

During one of our fights, I wrote him a letter pouring my heart out. I told him how much I loved and missed him. I was convinced that I had written a letter that would cause him to say, *"You are right, we belong together, I am sorry. Will you go out with me again?"*

Instead, the following words were blurred in my tear-filled eyes:

Cassidy,
Why can't we just be good friends? If I go out with you again, I would probably lose my

friends again. I really don't want that to
happen. I would rather be really close friends
and maybe I can ask you out again someday. If
one of us goes out with someone else then forget
it, okay?
Danny

I didn't want to be just friends! What did he mean 'other people'? Did he already have a new girlfriend lined up? I pulled out my records, put on a sad one, sat and cried until no tears were left.

Liz, was really tired of hearing about Danny and seeing me so down. She convinced me to go to the mall with her to get my mind off things with Danny. My dad called Liz 'Jabber Jaws.' She loved to talk and was very outgoing. In that sense, we were total opposites. Liz was a little taller than I with naturally curly hair. She totally hated it, especially when it was humid out. Our trip to the mall ended with me meeting a boy at the bus stop. His name was Kyle and we seemed to instantly hit it off. He had blond hair and blue eyes. He wasn't much taller than me and he had a very thin build. My heart still loved Danny but since he didn't love me anymore or want to be with me, I knew I had to move on. I also knew it wasn't going to be easy.

Then one day, a chance meeting with Danny's brother at our local deli led to me finding out that Danny asked another girl out.

Then the next day at school, his brother pointed her out to me. Her name was Kate. She was tiny like me and had dark hair like me. I instantly hated her. How could he get over me so quickly? *I have to give Kyle a chance,* my inner voice told me. *Danny doesn't care about you, so why care about him?*

My relationship with Kyle was far different from what I had with Danny. We spent a lot of time walking around, talking. We didn't write letters back and forth. We had a very simple relationship. But I found myself constantly wondering if Danny missed me like I missed him still.

One day before I'd introduced Kyle to my parents, a ring of the phone put my mind in a mixer. I just knew it was Danny. He was going to tell me that he was wrong and we should get back together. I ran to my stoop and waited for him. One look at his face told me that it wasn't a 'get back together' meeting.

"I heard you have a boyfriend?" he snapped at me.

"Sort of—well, you have a new girlfriend already!" I exclaimed right back at him.

"So, it is true?" His voice had a softer tone.

"You don't love me anymore and you already have a new girlfriend, right?" It was out there now, as my tears were slowly finding their way out of my eyes. I didn't want to cry. I wanted him to think I was fine. I didn't want him to know that not a single day went by that my thoughts didn't wander to him.

"I do love you! But that doesn't matter anymore, does it? And yes, I sort of have met someone..." He trailed off.

"If you loved me you wouldn't keep hurting me," I whispered.

"I think maybe we're just too young right now," he softly responded.

I didn't know what I was supposed to say. Maybe he did still love me? I couldn't answer him. Nothing was going to change the fact that we both obviously had moved on, or did we really?

"I will always love you, always and forever," he stated in a soft voice as he slowly turned and began walking back toward his house.

"I will always love you too, forever and always!" I managed to get out in between the sobs that were now full-steam. A long blink of my tear-filled eyes and he was gone. It was the first time my forever and always didn't make us smile.

~* * * *~

I knew what I had to do, and that was to put Danny out of my life. I would go out with Kyle and do everything in my power to not think of Danny anymore. It hurt too much to keep hoping and praying that he would come back to me. It was clear now that he had someone else....I just didn't want to cry anymore.

Before I knew it, months had flown by and I had managed to live through them. Danny stayed away from places where we would run into each other, and I did the same. That was until one day, we ran into each other at the deli.

I wanted to turn around and run out the door, but I had to be strong and not let him know that just seeing his face was making my heart pound so loudly. I felt sure everyone could hear it. One look at his face and I was off in that world where I believed we still had a chance.

"Hey," he said.

I studied his face hoping for a sign that he was happy to see me. "How are you doing?" Did he break up with that girl? Maybe we could get back together?

"I'm fine. I'll wait for you and we can walk back together," he replied in a voice that could melt my brain cells.

I finished with my order and there he was sitting outside the store, waiting for me.

"How are you and what's his face?" he asked.

"We're fine, I guess." I didn't want to talk about my boyfriend. I wanted to hear that he missed me!

"Want to go to a movie tonight?" he asked me in a rush of words, as if he didn't ask fast enough he might change his mind.

"Sure," was out of my mouth before I could even think about what it meant. I didn't want to ask about his girlfriend. I was afraid of what he might tell me. I didn't even give Kyle a moment's thought.

We made plans to meet at the corner of my street at 8:00 p.m. I was on cloud nine. I thought he was going to ask me to break up with my boyfriend and get back together with him.

It seemed that 8:00 pm took forever in coming. When it was time, I walked out my door and there in the middle of my street stood Danny. He looked so good and I realized just how very much I had missed him. But it was really hard to figure out what to talk about. We were both avoiding what was really happening between us.

"Do you miss me?" I just had to ask. Then I instantly regretted putting the words out there.

"Of course I do. I think about you all the time," he answered without any hesitation.

I was yelling at myself in my head. *Don't do it, and whatever you do, do not ask him if he wants to get back together. Do not ask him if he still loves you.* "I miss you too," was all I replied.

He took my hand and we walked without many words between us the rest of the way to the bus stop. We didn't have to wait long for the bus. We made our way to two seats in the back. I turned to look at him. I just needed to see those blue eyes that would melt me like butter in a hot pan. I'd forgotten just how very much I loved him. I was daydreaming when he leaned in to kiss me. I instantly responded to him. We kissed so passionately, in a way we never had before. A kiss that truly said I miss you and I love you.

When we stepped off the bus, he instantly grabbed my hand and we walked to the theatre. The movie could have been a blank screen for all I cared. It didn't matter what was on it. We spent the whole movie making out in the back anyway. When the movie ended all soon, we walked out holding hands and my head was reeling with questions about what would happen next.

We got on the bus to go back home, choosing seats in the back once again. We couldn't keep our hands off each other; our lips had never met so much. The bus ride home went way too quickly.

While we walked towards home, reality struck me dead-fast in the face when he uttered the following words to me, "You know I love you and miss you, but I hope you understand that I still don't think it will work for us right now. I think we need more time apart. Someday, maybe it will be the right time for us. I would still love to see you once in a while, but I am with Kate now and you have Kyle. I think this is for the best."

"What? Are you serious? Did you just use me?" I trembled as his words sliced through me like ice.

"I'm sorry, I thought you understood we're just good friends. We can still hang out with each other, just not as boyfriend and girlfriend officially."

"I don't know anything right now," I replied as my world was just pulled from beneath me, yet again. "I have to go. I will talk to you soon." I rushed into the house before he saw my tears.

I laid on my bed for a long time, not hysterical, just random tears rolling slowly down my cheeks and hitting the pillow. Did I want him part-time like this? Not being able to say he was my boyfriend but still seeing him and being with him? I convinced myself that having him occasionally would make him realize that we belonged together.

I was still really angry and with the help of Liz and Danny's brother, Dave, I found myself in his room being snoopy. I saw a giant glass jar filled with sunflower seeds, his favorite. His brother told me that Kate gave it to him as a present. When no one was looking, that giant jar wound up with cologne poured into it. Guess he wouldn't be eating those sunflower seeds. I knew it was childish, but I didn't care.

I continued my relationship with Kyle, and Danny continued to see Kate. I knew I should have felt remorse for being so dishonest with Kyle, but when it came to Danny, my mind only thought of him when he was around. I felt guilty for hurting Kyle but when I had a chance to be with Danny there was just no way my heart would say no. On Saturday nights, he went out with her and I went with Kyle. He and I then would meet up at my house and hang out until all hours of the night. We began to really talk for the first time in our relationship. We started to become really good friends, able to talk about everything. We even talked about Kyle and Kate at times. As much as we couldn't stay together as a couple, we weren't able to stay apart for long either.

My parents were either extremely trusting or very naïve as to what went on under their noses. We were allowed to hang out in my bedroom—something not allowed in my girlfriends' bedrooms with their boyfriends. We were allowed, I think initially, because there was no place else to go other than to be in the living room with my parents or sit in my kitchen. They trusted me. There were times when my mother walked in on us. It could be 100 degrees and he would be under a sleeping bag. One time, she came in, sat on the end of the bed and chatted with us. She never had any idea that he wasn't fully dressed under that blanket.

Then one day—the phone rang once. My heart instantly skipped a beat. I ran to the mailbox and found a letter.

Cassidy,
I need to see you tonight. I have some very bad news that I need to tell you about. It has to be tonight because tomorrow I will not be here. Meet me on the corner at 8:00 p.m.
Love, Danny

What? What could he possibly have to tell me and where was he going? We hadn't seen each other that much lately. I couldn't imagine what this could be about. I just wanted it to be 8:00, so I could find out. My nerves were shot while I sat and waited. I went up to my room, put on some 45s, stared out the window, and waited. *You Light Up My Life* clicked on. There was something about this song that always made me think of him and how no matter what happened between us, something about him always made my life better.

I became so impatient, I left my house a little early, hoping he would be early too, but he wasn't. I stood on the corner waiting for him. It seemed like hours, but was probably only a few minutes. At last, I saw him walking toward me, but not coming from his house. I wanted to run to him but I knew I couldn't seem overly anxious and I didn't know what this was all about.

"I'm leaving tomorrow," Danny stated in a voice that instantly told me this was bad. "I got a letter today from the school and I was kicked out. I burned it but they're going to call my parents. My dad is going to kill me. I'm going to go to Massachusetts." His parents' family friends lived there. There was a girl there close to our age. Her name was Brianna. I had heard about her a few times.

"Why can't you just talk to your parents?" I asked in a desperate voice. "I'm sure they can fix this and get you back in school."

"You don't understand. My dad is going to freak when he finds out. My dad can be really cool but when it comes to school…this will not go over well."

His explanation made me realize just how bad this situation truly was. I just didn't want him to leave. Even though we weren't together, it was nice knowing he was still close by. I also knew that if I really needed him, he would be there for me. What would I do if he decided to stay there?

I did understand it all and I just didn't want to admit it. I knew he had to run but I still wished there was another way.

"I'm taking the bus in the morning. I'll try to come back in a few weeks if I can. If I can't, I will do what I can to try to be here for your 16th birthday," he mumbled.

"I don't want you to leave!" I cried to him. His words kept echoing in my head. He was really leaving and I didn't know when I would see him again. He took me in his arms, which started full-blown tears to begin falling. In his arms, I always felt safe and his hugs made the worst day better.

"Don't make this any harder, please," he pleaded. "I have to do this. I'll try to come back for a visit soon, I promise." He pulled me into his arms again and gave me a really tight hug, then a long kiss. He walked away, then turned around for a second, and gazed into my eyes. "I love you, always and forever!"

Then—he was gone.

I don't know how long I stood there staring at the sky and asking why this was happening to me. I finally walked home and went straight to my room. I didn't want to talk to anyone and I couldn't tell anyone anyway, what was going on. I felt so alone. I grabbed the 45 of *Sad Eyes.* Then laid on my bed and cried.

The next night, Danny's mother called me. My mom answered the phone, her face looking confused. "Danny's mom wants to speak to you." My mom handed me the phone.

"Cassidy, I know you know where Danny went and what happened. Ray and David have told me most of what is going on. I know he saw you last night; do you know where he is?"

I wanted to lie, but if Ray and David had already told her, I knew I couldn't lie, and shouldn't. "He went to Massachusetts," I told her in a trembling voice. "He was scared about how you would react to him being thrown out of school." I felt instant relief. Maybe now, they would talk to him and he would come right back home.

"Thank you, Cassidy, for being so honest. Everything will be okay. His dad and I are going to call him later. At least we know he's safe. We were worried." With that, she said goodbye and hung up.

When I saw David the next day, he told me that his parents did call Danny the night before, but Danny wasn't coming back home. He was going to stay there for a while. I was crushed. All night, I kept thinking they would make him come back. Even though I knew he would be in trouble, at least he would be here again.

Weeks passed in a blur. I missed Danny and thought about him constantly. I played my sad 45s a lot, I guess too much, because a couple of them were skipping. I had to put a penny on the needle arm and that seemed to fix the problem for the time being.

~* * * *~

Before I knew it, my Sweet 16 party was finally on the horizon—that coming weekend. I could hardly wait. My girlfriend Beth was going to stay over for the weekend. I also couldn't wait to tell her everything that had been happening lately. Beth was the type of girl every guy instantly loved. She was short with blonde hair, blue eyes, and had the personality to fit her good looks. She was lots of fun to be around and had a heart of gold.

Beth used to live nearby. We met one night playing volleyball at a local recreation center and instantly became friends. She just recently moved with her family. It was really hard, not having her around like before, but we wrote each other several times a week. Luckily, her parents agreed to let her come for my birthday party. She came in on the bus and was able to spend the weekend with me. I wished she could have stayed longer. It was such a short visit but at least, she was there for my birthday.

Liz and Leslie came over early the day of the party to help me decorate. We went to the local hardware store and convinced them to go into their special storage area to find us Christmas lights. We spent all day hanging up the lights all around the room. I had bought a disco ball the week before, which I couldn't wait to use. It was a pain carrying all of my records downstairs, but it would be worth it.

Danny hadn't come back from Massachusetts, so he would not share my Sweet 16 birthday with me. I was so disappointed. I missed him so much, but he also probably wouldn't come because Kyle would be there. But I wasn't going to let my thoughts of him ruin my birthday.

Everyone arrived on time and my basement was filled with my friends. Kyle and his brother showed up. The music was really loud, the disco ball was spinning, laughter filled the room, and dancing filled the floor space available.

I was dancing with Kyle, when out of the corner of my eye, I saw Danny and his brother walking down the stairs. I knew David would definitely be there; he was anxious to see Beth again. But I couldn't believe my eyes. I couldn't believe Danny was here. I really didn't expect him to make it back for my party. From the second I saw him, I immediately fell back into that trap that he always seemed to catch me in. I managed to get Beth's attention, and she swiftly followed me upstairs.

"What am I going to do? Can you believe he showed up here, knowing Kyle would be here?" I blurted. "He did tell me he would try to be back for my party and he actually made it!" My excitement was in high gear.

"I know you still love him, you know that you can't fool me." She knew me too well. "I'm sure he won't start any trouble and ruin your party. Let's just see what happens. If I sense trouble, I'll get David to convince him to leave, okay?"

"Thanks! I sure do miss you being around. It will be nice to catch up when everyone leaves. Let's get back to the party now," I told her as my butterflies grew into dinosaurs now that Danny and Kyle were in the same place.

As I walked down the stairs, I heard counting.

"What's going on?" I asked, and then I saw Danny and Kyle on my basement floor. Oh no, this couldn't be good. As I got closer and could see better, it seemed that while I was upstairs they had decided to have a push-up match. I didn't know which of them started it, but it wasn't good. We all watched as this boy I so easily melted with and my new boyfriend battled for push-up champion. I felt really sorry for Kyle when Danny beat him at their game. I could tell by the look on Kyle's face he wasn't too happy that Danny was at the party, more so now that he just lost the challenge. I didn't understand why boys do dumb things like that. But I guess it could have been worse and they could have done something more violent than push-ups.

The party ended late. Kyle had to leave to catch a bus home. I knew he wasn't happy with the night's events. I walked him outside to say goodbye, dreading the inquisition I knew was about to come.

"Why aren't Danny and David leaving?" Kyle questioned me the second we were alone.

"David really likes Beth, and since she's leaving the day after tomorrow, he just wants to spend some more time with her. I'm sure they're going to leave very soon," I answered. I was anxious to get back inside and I really didn't want to fight with him.

"I don't know why Danny showed up here in the first place. He does know that we're going out, right?" Kyle asked me.

"Of course, he does. You have nothing to worry about, he has a girlfriend. We're just friends," I told him. As soon as the words were out of my mouth, I wondered if I sounded convincing.

"Well...I need to get going or my brother and I are going to miss the last bus. I'll call you tomorrow." He leaned over to give me a kiss goodnight, wished me a happy birthday again, and walked away.

I knew I would be questioned more the next day. Thank God, he had to catch the bus or I would've been forced to answer more questions. I couldn't explain why Danny made everything else in my life seem unimportant, but that was just the way it was.

When I walked back into the room, Danny smiled at me.

I knew he was proud of himself that he was able to beat Kyle.

David and Beth were deep in conversation on the couch.

Danny called me over. He reached into his pocket and handed me a tiny box. "Happy Birthday. Brianna helped me pick this out for you."

I truly hadn't expected a present from him. I wasn't happy hearing Brianna helped him either. I opened the box. Inside was a beautiful gold rose ring. I'd never seen anything so beautiful. I took it out of the box and put it on. I couldn't stop staring at it.

"Do you like it?" Danny asked.

"Like it? I love it!" My excitement was in overdrive. I gave him a hug and a kiss. He instantly grabbed me in a tight bear hug, one that I didn't want to end. It felt so good to be back in his arms again. My mind instantly began thinking that this was a sign that maybe he wanted to get back together. Why would he spend so much on me and come to my party if he didn't love me?

We stayed up most of the night just talking, kissing here and there. I didn't ask the question about getting back together. I also avoided what was going to happen about school. It didn't look like he was going back and would start working full-time for his dad.

It was 5:30 a.m. when he finally got up to go home. "What are you and Beth doing for her last night here?" he asked me.

"My dad offered to buy us a bottle of wine," I stated.

"Is it all right if David and I come over? I'm sure we can help you drink that," he joked.

"Sure!" I know I shouldn't have sounded so excited about that prospect, but knowing I would get to see him again made me so happy.

"Okay, I'll call you later. I hope you had a nice birthday." He pulled me into another tight hug, and gave me a kiss.

"It was the best birthday ever. Thank you so much for the ring, I love it! I will never take it off." I meant every word.

Beth had passed out a long time ago. I couldn't even remember when David left. When Danny was in my world, I remained in a place with only him.

I laid on my bed, staring at my ring, and praying that tomorrow would be just as wonderful as today.

~* * *~

The next night, Danny and David did come over. We drank the whole bottle of wine that my dad got us. I tried to teach Danny to dance. We had the time of our lives. We laughed so much while watching Danny try to dance drunk. He stayed over really late again. The conversation of getting back together was avoided. We just lived in the moment. Danny and David offered to come with me to take Beth back to Port Authority the next day to catch her bus back home.

We left early to catch the train to the city, which is where the bus station is. When we got to the train station, David wanted to run to White Castle real quick. He didn't make it back in time and missed the train. Beth looked really disappointed that she didn't get a chance to say goodbye to him. It was really sad seeing her leave again.

I truly had the best birthday weekend I could have ever dreamed of. I got to be with Danny all weekend. Once the weekend ended, life would go back to normal. Danny and I wouldn't get back together and I would continue to go out with Kyle. He wasn't happy about my being friends with Danny, though. I didn't know how I would ever explain the ring to him, but somehow I did.

The magic and color in my world disappeared again, as quickly as it had come for Danny and me.

~* * * *~

A few months later, a dozen roses arrived at my door, with a note from Danny saying that he was thinking of me. The roses reminded me of my ring, that I wore every day, and of the wonderful weekend when he gave it to me, when life was good. He was never far from my thoughts, but I also accepted that our chance encounters would not necessarily mean we were back together. We would meet, share a wonderful night together, and go back to our separate lives.

Kyle and I broke up. We decided we were better at being friends. He didn't like that I had a lot of guy friends, and he especially didn't like that I was friends with Danny. He lived in a different town and went to a different school, so getting together was always a problem too.

The weekend that Danny's brother was getting married arrived. Danny was in the groom's party. Since our families were so close, even though Danny and I weren't together, we were all invited to attend.

Before the wedding, Danny was in one of his bad moods, bragging to me about how Brianna would be there and he would be spending a lot of time with her. We got into a huge fight. I had figured he would be past it and in a good mood since it was his brother's wedding. But when I saw him at the wedding, I wasn't prepared for what followed. He was so drunk he could barely stand.

I was standing with my dad when Danny's words slapped me in the face.

"Your daughter is a slut," he said in a slurred voice.

I stood there with tear-filled eyes, not believing what I just heard him say.

His dad was close by and grabbed him by the arm.

I didn't know how my father restrained himself and didn't deck Danny right there. Then my father grabbed Danny's other arm and they pulled him into the elevator and disappeared.

Did he really feel that way about me? Why would he say something so horrible to me and to my dad?

My mom quickly came over to me and took me into the bathroom. We didn't speak— nothing could change the words I'd heard, and I don't think my mom knew what she could possibly say that could make what just happened better.

My dad didn't come back to the table for a while. When he did return, he told me that he and Danny's dad took Danny and got him sobered up. This was after Danny had barfed everywhere. It seemed they all were drinking in the limo, and no one was paying attention to just how much he was taking in.

Nothing mattered to me by then, except getting out of that place and getting as far away from Danny as I possibly could. I wouldn't even look at him. For the first time in our two years of knowing each other, I was so humiliated, infuriated, and confused. My mind was filled with thoughts that kept racing by, like *Why did he do this to me? How could he do this to me?* I was beyond embarrassed. I didn't know how I would ever get past it. That night, I cried myself to sleep.

The next day, a ring of the phone led me to find a letter in my mailbox. I knew it was him. I really didn't want to read it. I did not want to hear how sorry he was.

Cassidy,

I am really sorry for yesterday. I know you are not going to believe me. I couldn't sleep last night. I do not even remember all that happened but my brother told me what I said to your dad. I don't know why I would say something that horrible. You know I don't think that! I am going to come over later and apologize to your dad and you in person. I hope you will forgive me. I love you always and forever!

Danny

I made the decision right then and there that I wouldn't be home when he arrived. I called Leslie and made plans to hang out with her that night.

I found out later when I got back home, that Danny did stop over and talked to my parents. They also told me he seemed upset that I wasn't there, so he could apologize to me in person. Sorry just didn't erase the words that were said, not by someone who claimed to love me. Someone I had given my heart and soul to over and over. I made up my mind right then— I was done.

~* * * *~

David and a bunch of my friends all got tickets to go see Charlie Daniels at the Nassau Coliseum. We had to rely on his parents to drive us there and my parents were the ride home. Probably a good thing because they wouldn't freak if they realized we were a little buzzed. One of my friends snuck a wine sack in and we all drank some.

Halfway into the second song, I was looking around at all the people; the place was so crowded. Then my eyes stopped. *No! It couldn't be!* A couple rows ahead of me was Danny and right by his side, hanging on him, was Kate. I knew I shouldn't care, yet I could feel my temperature starting to boil. I wondered if he acted moody and nasty to her. The music kept playing but my eyes wouldn't stop staring at them. The next thing I knew, he was facing my way. *Does he see me? That's a dumb question. You know damn well, he sees you.* He smiled, waved to me, and turned back around. I tried really hard to concentrate on the concert and enjoy the show. My friend Liz tapped me on my shoulder, which brought me out of the trance I must have been in.

"Check out the new guy, his name is Chaz!" She was giddy from the wine and would have liked nothing more than to hear me stop complaining to her about Danny every day.

"I met him at school the other day," I replied. He wasn't bad looking but I wasn't sure I wanted to go out with anyone just yet. He had a dark complexion, dark brown hair, and charcoal eyes. Between Kyle and Danny, I was done with dealing with boys.

"Well, I just heard him tell Christopher that he likes you and wants to ask you out," she babbled to me. "You really should go out with him. You truly need to get over Danny once and for all."

I didn't want to get over Danny, deep down. No matter how hard I tried, thoughts of him constantly filled my mind. I didn't go out with the new boy. We did hang out with the same people, and I did see him a lot, but I needed the time to myself.

Time moved on and the holidays arrived and left as quickly as they always do. I did agree to meet Danny one night. We didn't talk about the past. In no time at all, it seemed like nothing bad ever happened between us. I didn't understand how I could still love him. On weekends, we would occasionally wind up together late at night.

I thought I had finally realized that life with Danny was like an impending hurricane. One minute, things could be good and happy and then in a fleeting moment, it would be gone.

CHAPTER SIX

1980 – Age 17

A Burger King was built right by our school. Liz and I both applied and got jobs there. Opening day was New Year's Day. I arrived at work very excited. I was looking forward to working there. Liz and I would hopefully have the same shifts. The manager handed me a uniform and I went downstairs to get changed. When I returned, I saw something I couldn't believe. There, already in a uniform, was Danny! Somehow, neither of us told the other that we were going to work there. Why did our paths always seem to cross? Did fate have to keep putting us in the same place? The day went so fast, it was so busy, there wasn't time to worry about Danny. As soon as my shift ended, I left. I didn't look around for Danny. My mom was there to pick me up and drive me home.

A couple of days later, Danny bought his first car and went to my house to show me. He called it the Arabian. I didn't know cars, so I had no idea what kind of car it was. All I knew was now he had the freedom to go places. I couldn't wait until I got my license and my first car. It would be a great feeling to be able to go where I wanted.

"Feel like taking a ride?" he asked me.

"Sure! Where do you want to go?" Not that I really cared. I was just happy to be going for a ride.

"Let's go to Jack in the Box, then we can just drive around the harbor," he replied.

"Okay, let me grab my jacket and tell my parents I'm going out." I headed to the door. I didn't give my parents a chance to question me too much.

We went to Jack in the Box and I ordered a hamburger. Afterward, we drove around and pulled over in a deserted area. It was barely a minute before we began making out. It'd been a really long time since we had kissed. There was a sense of urgency between us that wasn't there before. Nothing had changed for us, though. We had a wonderful evening together, but it was just another memory and reminder that it was something I didn't really have.

~* * * *~

Time moved swiftly for me. The boy from the Charlie Daniels concert asked me to go out with him. I decided to say yes. It was nice to have a boyfriend again. He was friends with all the same people I was, something Danny and I didn't share. There wasn't a worry that he would lose friends by hanging out with me all the time.

Right by our high school was a pizza parlor that we visited daily, right next door to Burger King. Those places would get overcrowded during lunchtime. The businesses shared a huge parking lot, which was also the designated hang out spot for nights.

I don't know who brought the bottles of wine, but we were all drinking it. The couples in the group came up with an idea to put their names on the wall that was right by the pizza parlor. That way, everyone would see it. I decided to put my and Chaz' names on the wall in a heart. I knew Danny would see it. Then he would see that I had moved on.

The next day, I was anxious to see the artwork that we all created the night before. I walked up to the wall, but I might as well have been punched in the stomach when I saw "Danny and Kate, Always and Forever," right next to Chaz' and my names. He had used our phrase! That started a war of words on the wall between Kate and me. I saw her at school with the rest of her snooty friends, but we managed to stay out of each other's face. I wasn't sure what she knew about me, but I guessed she knew I was Danny's ex.

The war had begun. For the next few weeks, each day, new hearts with names and dates appeared on the wall. Before long, the wall was filled. I'm sure the pizza parlor knew who was filling the wall. We were in there enough, and they knew all of our names. They never said a word to us, though. When the wall could hold no more, the war of words was over, but our feelings towards each other lingered.

I knew I shouldn't have cared about Kate being with Danny. He was free to be with whomever he pleased, and I was with Chaz, but as much as we weren't together, I did not like the idea of him with someone else.

My phone rang once and soon Danny was sitting in my living room with me. Chaz and Kate were only briefly discussed. I think we both enjoyed the jealousy that our other relationships spiked in us. It was known by now that we were not getting back together. I worked really hard to keep the thoughts of us going out again, as far away as I possibly could. When he walked out the door hours later, a piece of me sneaked out beside him, undetected. His heart might have been with Kate, and mine with Chaz, but my soul always went with Danny. There was a deep yearning in my heart, that no matter what I did, no matter what I said, all I needed to do was see his face or hear his voice and I would be drawn right back into the world that I loved. Yet, it was a world filled with uncertainty and tears.

CHAPTER SEVEN

1981 – Age 18

Days blended together, and our lives had taken us separate ways. That didn't stop us from occasionally meeting up late at night some weekends. When we did, we always wound up staying up half the night talking, and sometimes making out, but things didn't change. We still continued to be with other people.

When Danny's car broke down on a trip to see his friends in college, he had to take a bus home to get money and go back. He asked me to go on the trip with him. I don't recall how or where I told my parents I was going, but I went for the ride. We had to take a Greyhound bus to get there. We sat in the back of the bus, flirting and making out the whole way there. We went to his sister's college and stayed the night with her. In the morning, we went to a small diner, had breakfast, and then started the journey back home. Wherever he got the car fixed, they didn't fix it right, and before long, the car started to really act up. We had to drive really slowly the rest of the way home.

When we got back, life continued the way it had been. We didn't get back together and we continued our separate, yet occasionally together lives.

On a night when I was with Chaz, we had a fight and I wanted to leave. In an instant, I called Danny to rescue me. He didn't hesitate and told me he was on his way. In the meantime, Chaz and I worked things out, and he begged me to stay. There was no way to reach Danny to tell him not to come. I made the decision to pick a fight with Danny rather than tell him the truth that I wanted to stay. He got so mad, he punched a street sign and split his knuckles open. I felt horrible as I watched him drive away. I never told him the real reason I picked a fight, since with us fighting was common.

Chaz and I ended up breaking up for good shortly after that night anyway. We continued to wind up in the same places as we shared all the same friends. It was really hard and awkward. I wanted him back, more so, I believe, because I didn't want to be alone.

I went out with my girlfriends to clubs in hopes of finding someone new. I knew in my heart that Danny and I were just good friends. He had made it clear too many times. Yet, whenever I needed help, Danny was the first person I always thought of to call.

A night out at the Oak Beach Inn, which was a dance club, would find my friend and me stuck with no way home. The guys we went with were complete assholes and left my friend and I stranded there. We were far from home and I wasn't about to call my parents to pick us up. I made the decision yet again, to call upon Danny to rescue me.

He drove all the way out there and brought me safely home, never questioning why he was the one I called.

~* * * *~

I still wanted to get back with Chaz, although I really didn't know why. I believe it was because it was nice to have a boyfriend who was friends with all the same people. Since David and I hung out with the same people, he tried to help me make that happen. It didn't work.

Time moved on and before we knew it, it was time to start making plans for prom. It became clear that there was no way that I was going with Chaz. David and I decided to go together to prom. I knew there was no way that Danny would agree to go with me and I didn't want to go alone. David and I were really good friends, so it seemed to be the logical solution.

Prom weekend came and went quickly after all the preparation for it. David and I had a great time. After the prom, we drove to Montauk Point with all our friends to watch the sunrise. We stayed there for a while and then headed back home. After we all changed and slept for a while, we went to New Jersey to Great Adventure to end our weekend.

~* * * *~

It was summer again, but this time I needed to move into the real world. I found a job in town at a microfilming place. On my first day, I met someone. His name was George. We stared at each other most of the day. He wasn't what I would call great-looking, but he wasn't ugly either. He had light brown hair parted on the side with a sort of swoop, reminding me of a 50s hairstyle. He was a few inches taller than I was and had a medium build.

I also met a girl named Crystal. She started working there a few weeks before I did, so they had her help me that day. She was really easy to talk to. It was like an instant connection. I found myself telling her a lot about myself and learned a lot about her as well. I found out she had a boyfriend and she thought that I should give George a chance, should he ask me. Funny, how in a short time she was another one who thought I needed to give up on Danny.

It was near the end of the workday when just that happened. George approached me and said, "Would you like to go out to dinner tonight? I know of a really nice Italian place we can go to if you're not busy."

"Sure, I would love to," I replied, trying not to seem too anxious. It was the first time I would be going out with someone in what seemed like a long time.

"What's your address and phone number? I can pick you up about 7:00, if that gives you enough time to get ready?" he added.

"Seven will be fine." I wrote my address and number on a piece of paper and handed it to him.

We went to a really nice restaurant I'd never been to before. Talking to him was easy. We had a wonderful dinner. I think I may have just experienced the first time in years that I didn't think of Danny for an entire night. After dinner, we pulled up in front of my house and sat in his car for hours, talking. He told me that he lived with his brother; his family lived in Chicago. When I noticed the time and realized we both needed to get up early the next day for work, we decided it was time to say goodnight.

"Thank you so much for dinner!" I told him. "I had such a nice time tonight."

"Will you go out with me?" he asked me in a shy voice.

"Yes!" I replied without a second thought.

He leaned over to my side of the car and gave me a quick kiss goodbye. I got out of the car and went inside. I went to my room and replayed the evening in my head. I couldn't believe how great the night had been. George was so different from the other guys I'd met. He was secure and knew what he wanted.

I found myself falling in love and truly happy for the first time in a very long time.

Christmas came and went. George gave me a beautiful bracelet with a heart. He had our initials engraved on the back of it. He got along with everyone in my family he had met. I ignored the fact that he didn't seem to know when it was time to stop drinking.

I found out that Danny and Kate broke up but I didn't even think about going out with him. I did occasionally meet up with Danny as we talked and reminisced. He knew I had a new boyfriend and that I was serious about him, but it didn't seem to bother him.

CHAPTER EIGHT

1982 – Age 19

A New Year was when new hopes and dreams began. I got to see George every day at work and we saw each other most nights. We didn't fight like Danny and I did, so life was peaceful.

George surprised me with tickets for Air Supply. He knew how much I loved their love songs. Everything about the night was perfect in every way. I knew every song by heart and enjoyed every second of the show.

We seemed to glide through the months without drama until a day in June when a phone call changed my safe world.

"What are you doing?" a familiar voice that always melted me asked.

It'd been months since we had seen or talked to each other. Yet, those few simple words made my heart flutter instantly. "Nothing, just listening to music, why?" I was instantly curious as to why he was calling me after all this time, and calling me without even putting a letter in the box first.

"Can I come over?" he asked.

"Yeah," I answered, probably too quickly. "I'm upstairs in my room, listening to music." It's a good thing that George was going out with his brother that night. I wouldn't have wanted to have to lie to him to find a way to see Danny.

Was it moments, seconds, minutes or an eternity since he called? Time seemed to have decided not to move. I couldn't imagine why he wanted to come over after all this time. I heard my front door open and close. I heard his voice talking to my parents. My heart wouldn't stop pounding in my chest, anticipating why he wanted to come over.

I tried to find something to keep me busy, so I started going through my record pile, finding a song to put on my stereo. I was deep in thought when his voice snapped me back to reality.

"I got this for you," he told me as he handed me a cute teddy bear that had the words, *I Miss You* on it.

Sad Eyes was once again playing in the background. My mind couldn't seem to think straight or even come out with words to respond. "You miss me?" This was all I could come up with to respond. After all this time and all these months, when I had finally moved on and was happy, now he missed me?

"Yes," he whispered. "I haven't been able to stop thinking about you lately. I really miss you. I want you back!" He hesitated for a moment and then said, "I love you."

All those feelings I had put behind me came crashing down on me. I think I just left my body and was watching from above like in a dream. He wasn't really here telling me this, right? I hadn't heard him say that he loved me in so long. Nope, he was still there and I didn't know what to do.

He pulled me closer and began to hug me really tight. A soft kiss lingered on my lips. I still couldn't even speak. We started to make out and I didn't know how to stop. I didn't know if I wanted to stop. Being with him after being apart for so long, reminded me just how much I loved being wrapped in his arms and how much I loved his lips against mine. The hickey that resulted from our night of passion would be a serious problem, though. I didn't know how on earth I was going to explain that one to George. It wasn't like I could avoid him—we did work together.

I told Danny that I needed time to think it all through, because I was afraid to go back with him and wind up breaking up again. After he left, I tried to work it out in my mind, until my mind felt ready to explode and just shut off.

I managed to cover the hickey and faced George at work. I felt like shit. I knew I had to make a decision and it was one I didn't want to have to make. I told him that I wasn't feeling good to avoid too many questions. I figured if he thought I was sick he wouldn't ask me what was wrong. It also got me out of having to see him that night.

As soon as I got home from work, I put in an SOS call to Liz. She would help me figure this mess out. She understood my relationship with Danny and knew that as much as I said I had moved on and thought I had, the love Danny and I shared went way too deep.

She arrived at my door with a box of tissues in hand. The girl knew the rain was going to come. I told her calmly all the events of the last 24 hours. She didn't interrupt, but did what I needed her to do—just listen and not judge.

"I think you need to be fair to George," Liz advised. "Are you sure Danny really wants to get back together and are you sure that is what you want to do? You have been so happy lately, do you want to risk that again by going back to Danny?" She handed me a tissue.

I knew all her words were true. "I know— it's just so hard." My tears began to fall quite freely now. "I think I love George, but my love for Danny is just—just so different. My feelings for Danny are just—you know what I am saying, right?" I could barely talk at that point, so I was praying she got it.

She was my best friend so of course, she understood as she handed me another tissue. "I do understand, but I just don't want to see you get hurt again," Liz stated in her best-friend with-sympathy voice. "I know how badly Danny ripped your heart out last time. You know whatever you decide or whatever happens, I will be there with a box of tissues. Maybe you should take some time and really think about this. Talk to Danny, be sure this is what he really wants and that he's not just playing games with you."

I knew she was right. Danny might have already changed his mind by then. I could ruin what I had with George and wind up without either of them. I rang Danny's phone once and waited for him to respond. A minute later, my phone rang. We met outside.

"I spent all night and day thinking about what you told me." My words seemed to hang in the air. "I know I love you with all my heart, but—I know our history. I would love nothing more than to be your girlfriend again. I just need to know that this is real and that this is truly what you want, too."

"I told you last night, I miss you! We have had so many good times together. I love you and I want to be with you," he responded.

"I want to believe you, and part of me does believe you, but I am scared of getting hurt again," I explained. "You know I'm with someone else and I don't want to give that up and then wind up losing you again too."

"That's not going to happen," he tried to convince me. "We are older now and I really think things will be better for us now."

Every single part of me wanted to believe this more than anything in the world, but did I?

He pulled me into his arms, our eyes met. Our eyes spoke in ways that meant no words needed to be said.

When he left, I began to devise my plan to break up with George. I knew that my heart belonged to Danny and I had to try to make it work with him. I decided that the truth was what I needed to tell George. I am an honest person and I just didn't want to lie to George. He deserved the truth. I did care about him but I had to follow my heart and see where it took me.

George's reaction wasn't what I thought it was going to be. He was upset but also seemed to understand. He wanted me to be happy and if I believed that I could have that with Danny then he was willing to let me go.

I quit my job. It was just too hard to face George every day after what I'd done. I would find a new one where I wouldn't have to face someone I hurt so badly. Crystal was so upset that I quit, she said work wasn't the same without me there. She was soon thinking of quitting and getting a different job.

I walked over to my jewelry box, gently opened it, and gazed inside. There sitting exactly where I left it was my ankle bracelet from Danny. I didn't wear it on my ankle, but instead attached it to a chain and wore it around my neck. I wanted everyone to see it. It was now official—I was back with Danny. As I stared at myself in the mirror and looked at my ankle bracelet, I realized just how badly I wanted this. Deep down, I knew but it wasn't until that moment, when I could put it back on that reality really hit me.

On our first official date back together, we decided to go to the drive-in and see *Fast Times at Ridgemont High*. It was so easy for us. We picked up right where we left off as if no time apart had occurred.

We became a couple in ways that we'd never been before. We went to his brother's for parties. When we were asked how long we were together, we always said five years; it was as if we never were really apart. We talked about getting engaged sometime next year. Things were the way I believed they truly should be.

Four months later—everything changed for me. All of a sudden, Danny wasn't calling me when he was supposed to. He was going out with his friends a lot and I was left to wonder what was happening. I felt so confused. I wished he would talk to me when he had a problem. If I was the one he was going to spend the rest of his life with, he should be able to talk to me about anything. I really hoped Danny and I could find a way to communicate better when things weren't good. When I questioned him, he told me not to worry, that everything was fine and we would be married in about a year from then.

I was still worried though. Something didn't seem right with Danny lately. He was hanging around with someone whom I believed was doing drugs. I questioned him and he told me that he wasn't.

"Let's go away for the weekend," Danny said to me. "I think we could use some time alone, what do you think?"

"Where do you want to go?" I was really excited. This could be a chance for us to really have some time alone.

"Let's go to Lake George. I think we can find a place not too expensive there and we'll go for the weekend."

"I love the idea! Let's do it." I was already thinking about what I should pack. I also wondered what my parents would say about this. I didn't really care if they weren't happy about it; I wasn't a child anymore. I could go away with Danny if I wanted to.

We spent the rest of the week finding a place to stay and getting our stuff together to bring. My parents' reaction wasn't what I anticipated. They didn't freak out or give me a hard time.

The day arrived, the car was all packed up, and we started our weekend journey together finally.

"Let's stop in Rockaway, get a little pot for the trip," he told me. "We won't get much, just so that we can smoke a little together, okay?"

"Umm, I guess so," I answered hesitantly. I didn't want to argue about this and I guessed it would be all right.

"We'll stop at the bicycle store."

"A bicycle store sells pot?" I never heard of the place but obviously, he had and must have gone there before. I wasn't happy about it but I just wanted to get away. I also didn't want to ruin our trip by starting a fight with him about it.

We pulled over and he got out of the car. "I'll be right back, just stay here in the car." He then crossed the street to go into the store.

I was listening to music on the radio, deep in thought and dreaming about our trip, when in an instant, my car door was swung open. My heart started racing. *What the hell is going on?* In a split second, a knife was on my neck. Then a large hand grabbed the necklace from around my neck and snapped it off.

A firm voice told me, "Give me your pocketbook right now, and be quick!"

It was dark and I was afraid to move, afraid to think, and too scared to even look at who was there. I was completely frozen in time. I quickly handed him everything I had and in a blink of an eye, he disappeared. I was afraid to even close the car door. I didn't want to move. I was frozen in shock. What if he was watching me and decided to come back? I finally got the courage, reached over quickly to close the door, and locked it. I leaned over and began pushing the horn. I didn't let go, just let it honk. I wasn't even thinking about all the attention I was bringing to myself at that point. My tears began to fall and hysteria took over. I couldn't even see because my tears were falling too quickly.

All of a sudden, there was a loud bang on the window. I didn't want to look. What if he was back and thought I didn't give him everything? The banging continued and I heard Danny's voice.

"It's me. Let me in, what happened?" His voice sounded scared.

It was hard to talk, I was so scared, and just wanted to get out of there. "I w-was—robbed," I managed to say as my hysteria continued.

"WHAT?" He was at a complete loss for words, too. It was minutes before he spoke again, "Tell me what happened. Are you okay? Are you hurt?"

I began shaking uncontrollably. I kept reliving the knife at my throat. I could be dead right now. My necklace and all my money were gone. "How am I going to explain this to my parents? I can't very well tell them we were in Rockaway buying pot. I need to tell them something happened." I knew if I didn't come up with something good, I would never get to see Danny again. Even though I wasn't a child, I lived under their roof and life would be hell if they knew what really happened.

We got out of Rockaway as quickly as we could. We pulled over and began to work out a plan to explain what just happened. We knew I had to tell them I was robbed. A total cover-up plan was created. I felt guilty for having to lie about it but also knew the trouble I would be in if I told the truth. The details about the knife were best left out of the cover-up plan.

We got back to my house and the moment I walked in the door, my parents saw my face and instantly knew something terrible just happened.

Still crying, I explained that I was just robbed at a local store in the parking lot and that they took my pocketbook and necklace. My parents went into action, called the police without hesitation, and everyone went to the scene of the crime. They combed the area hoping this person who robbed me decided to drop my bag after he took the money out. My stomach was turning upside down. I hated lying.

I always tried to be as honest as I could be. I felt so guilty about everyone looking for my stuff when I knew it was nowhere near, where we were searching. After hours of searching, it became clear that my bag would not be found.

"What should we do about Lake George?" Danny asked me. "I feel awful about this and totally responsible. It's up to you. I have plenty of money if you still feel like going."

"I want to get out of here! I can't sit around here and keep rehashing the lies I just told."

We managed to convince my parents that going away was a good idea. I needed to get away even just for the couple of days. Danny explained to them that I wouldn't need money, he would take care of me.

I decide not to even write about this in my diary. If I didn't tell anyone, maybe I could convince myself that it wasn't true. We got to Lake George really late. Luckily, they held our reservation for us. The weekend trip was just what I needed to get my mind off the recent events. We played miniature golf and enjoyed some private time that we didn't seem to have often.

It wasn't long before we had to get back to reality. Danny and I seemed to be drifting apart. I was tired of his moods and not calling when he said he would. I began to think of how I didn't have this problem with George. I thought Danny was doing drugs much more than I knew about and I was just not important enough to him right then.

I couldn't believe I was going to do this. After long conversations with Leslie and Liz, I decided I must break up with him and see if I could save my relationship with George. That was going to be the hardest thing I'd ever done, yet I knew it was what I needed to do. I knew that if I faced Danny and tried to tell him I would chicken out. I decided to write him a letter.

Dear Danny,
This is truly the hardest letter I have ever had to write to you. I really believed when we got back together that things would be different for us. I thought that we had both gotten older and we could have the relationship that I always thought we should have. The last couple of weeks you have proven me wrong. You don't call me when you say you will and don't even want to see me that often. I need someone who wants to be there for me and is there for me. I love you more than I have ever loved anyone in my life, but I just can't do this anymore. I feel like there is something else going on that you're not telling me about. I am sorry that it has come to this and I will miss you so much!

Please don't write back or call; it will be too hard to talk.

Love, Forever & Always,

Cassidy

I folded the paper stained with my tears, put it in his mailbox, rang his phone once, and shut the door once again on my life with Danny. Deep down, I hoped that he would do exactly what I said not to. I hoped he would call or write me a letter that melted my cold heart, but he didn't. It was really over once again.

After a week of wallowing in self-pity and feeling as if my heart was in pieces, I decided to call Leslie, Liz, and Crystal. We all had become really good friends. They arrived shortly after, Liz with a tissue box in hand. We joked about the tissues. Luckily, that night I didn't need them. We decided a girls night out was in order. I wasn't looking to meet anyone else, just needed a night out to keep my mind off my broken heart.

We arrived at McQuades, got a nice booth, ordered some shots, and our night began. My friends did a good job helping me cheer up. The last thing I expected that night was to see George and his brother walk in.

"Hey," George said with a smile on his face.

"Hi," I replied. I began to feel bad about how I betrayed him.

"How are you doing? Can we go outside and talk for a minute?" he hesitantly asked me.

"Sure, I guess so," I answered. I gave Crystal, Liz, and Leslie a look that only girlfriends understand. I didn't want to go over all that had happened. I also didn't want to explain how I was wrong by giving Danny another chance.

We walked outside and began small talk. I knew Danny's name was going to come up in the conversation and I avoided it as long as I possibly could. I looked at George and remembered all the good times we had together. I just didn't want to make another mistake.

"You know I have to ask you how you and Danny are," he muttered.

"We're not together anymore. Honestly, I don't want to talk about it. I came here with my friends to have a good time," I explained to him.

"I understand…I can't say I am sorry to hear this, though," he quietly responded. "Maybe when you're up to it and feel ready we can go out to dinner and talk? I really have missed you."

There it was, those words I didn't want to hear, and didn't deserve to hear after what I did to him. "I need time, but I will call you and we will go out one night, okay?" I just wanted to get back inside to my friends and my girls night. I couldn't go down that road, not tonight.

"Okay," he mumbled in a clearly disappointed voice.

"I am sorry, it is just too soon right now. Let's go back inside. Have a drink with us." I was desperate to get back inside to safety.

"I won't bother you and your friends. When you're ready, you call me," he stated and walked away.

I stood there staring at his back as tears began to fall. No, dammit, why do I have to cry all the time? I felt so bad for him. I knew he loved me, and I felt like such an idiot, but it was just too soon after Danny to even think about what I thought George wanted. I pulled myself together, went back inside, and climbed into the booth.

Everyone was anxiously waiting for the details.

I looked around and didn't see George anywhere. "Did he leave?"

"Yeah," Leslie replied. "He looked kind of upset. They left right after he came back in."

I told them what he said and how I responded. I tried not to think about him the rest of the night and to focus on our girls' night. I found myself thinking of the disappointment on his face, though.

We left shortly after and went back to my house. My parents were out, so we had the house to ourselves. We raided the kitchen, gathered up snacks and drinks, then sat up half the night chatting.

The next morning, we decided to go to the mall. Going to the mall and buying something is always good to help you feel better. As we were getting ready to leave, the doorbell rang.

There standing on my stoop was a flower deliveryman with a bouquet of flowers. "Cassidy? Sign here." He handed me the clipboard to sign for them.

I couldn't move fast enough to open the card.

Dear Cassidy,
I hope you will find it in your heart to call me and go to dinner with me.
Love, George

"Oh, my God," I cried. "I can't believe he sent me flowers."

My feeling of amazement was reflected on all my friend's faces.

"I think you need to go have that dinner with him," Crystal told me.

"Yes…I know you're right. I will tell him when I call to thank him. I just don't want to jump into anything, you know?"

I knew breaking up with Danny was the right thing to do but that didn't stop me from thinking about him, wondering what he was doing. Was he thinking of me? Did he miss me at all? My heart and soul missed him with every ounce of my being. I also knew I had to move forward. Why not with George? He really seemed to care about me, and he did treat me well when we went out. I had to be honest with him. I was sure he wasn't going to like what I knew I had to say. No matter what I did, no matter what I said, deep down I would always love Danny. He was my first love and the first person I gave my heart to. As much as I was not happy with the way things seemed to go for us, he would always in some way, be a part of my life. I dreaded this conversation but I knew I had to be honest with George and myself.

I made plans to go out with George and talk. I spilled my guts, cried a few tears, and awaited his response to all I had just shared with him.

"You're not going to go back to him again, are you?" he asked

"No, I really don't see that happening. I just need you to understand. We just don't work together but I do think that we'll be friends again someday. Our families are so close, I know I will see him, and I also know I can't ignore him forever. I know this isn't what you want to hear, but I don't want to hurt you."

"I love you, you know that, right?" he asked me.

"I know…I love you, too," I was hoping it sounded convincing. I did love him, or I believed I loved him, that much is true.

After what seemed like a long hesitation, he continued, "Will you go out with me again?" His words seem to linger in the air.

"Yes, I will go out with you again."

He leaned across the table and softly kissed me. He had the biggest smile on his face and it instantly warmed my cold heart.

~* * * *~

George and I shared the holiday season together; Christmas was wonderful. We went into the city, saw the Christmas tree and then took a horse and buggy ride. We rang in the New Year at a club with most of my friends. Things were about as perfect as they could be, except his heavy drinking at times did concern me.

We enjoyed each other's company and cherished our time together. We shared many romantic dinners at the Villa Rosa and long talks at our favorite wine and cheese café. He began talking about marriage and sharing the rest of our lives together. He told me that he was going to be asking my parents' permission soon and wanted to get engaged. He went on to say that he saw the ring he was getting me and had already been making payments on it.

When I questioned him more about it, he wouldn't elaborate. He said I would find out more when the time was right.

Crystal finally got her own apartment. I was so jealous. I loved going to her new place. We didn't have to worry about parents being around.

CHAPTER NINE

1983 – Age 20

My phone rang once. My heart began to beat faster and I was filled with an excitement I knew I shouldn't have. I practically fell over my own two feet to get to the mailbox to see what Danny had left there.

Dear Cassidy,
I know it has been a while and I don't really expect you to forgive me for what happened. I am just hoping that maybe we can at least be friends again. It would be really nice to see you and talk. If you don't want to, I understand, but I miss our friendship.
Love, Danny

Why? Why did he want to be friends now? He hadn't tried to talk to me since we broke up. Why, when my life was on a certain path and moving forward did my past come back to me?

George would flip out if he found out about this. There hadn't been any mention of Danny for a long time, and he probably thought I'd totally gotten over Danny once and for all. Even though in the back of my mind, there were still so many days when I went over the past in my head. I never told anyone about it, but I knew Danny would hold a place in my heart forever. I also tried hard to keep reality in check. Even though I believed that we really loved each other, we just didn't work together.

It was against my better judgment, but I agreed to meet him one night to talk. I just didn't know how to say no to him.

I wasn't inside my house more than five minutes when I heard a light knock at my front door. I hesitated for a split second before I opened it. There he was, standing in front of me, and in a flash my heart filled with a warmth I believed would be absent. I wanted him to hold me. I wanted his lips on mine. I was so angry with myself that I couldn't stop falling into the same trap.

We sat on the couch and he instantly began to talk about how much he'd been thinking about me. How much he missed me. He told me he was sorry for what happened and that it was his fault. "I just want us to be friends again. I know that I hurt you really bad but not a day goes by that I don't think about you and miss you."

His words sounded genuine, and I so wanted to believe they were. "We can only be friends. I'm back with George and we're really happy. We're actually talking about getting engaged. I can be your friend, I will always be your friend, but—it just can't be more than that again." There I said it. It was so hard to say, but I couldn't risk losing it all again.

"I understand. Wait—what do you mean you're talking about getting engaged?" he asked.

"Since we got back together, things are really good between us. He told me that he has picked out a ring. He won't tell me more. He said he's going to speak to my parents." Why was this so hard to say to him? I glanced over at him and a sadness I'd never seen before covered his face. I immediately looked away.

It seemed like a long time passed before he spoke again, "I thought you told me he drinks too much?"

"He does at times," I hesitantly replied. I didn't dare tell him that the previous week George was so drunk that my dad found him passed out in his car in front of my house. I drank too much sometimes too, so who was I to judge? I did worry that at times George didn't know when to stop, especially times when I didn't think it was appropriate to get drunk.

I thought Danny was waiting for me to say more but I didn't. I couldn't let him know that I had doubts. I found a movie for us to watch and the discussion about George ended as quickly as it started.

His hand reached mine and he grabbed it tightly…I didn't let go. He didn't need to say anymore; I knew I'd just broken his heart. When the movie ended, we knew it was time to say goodbye. Why did I feel so sad?

"Am I allowed to give you a hug and kiss goodbye?" he jokingly asked me, as he was pulling me closer. At times, I didn't think he knew how to be serious. He used jokes to mask his true feelings.

"Yes," I managed to say as my mind filled with thoughts of it being the last moment like this we would share. The feel of his arms around me, the look of loss in his eyes, and his lips wrapped up in mine engulfed me. I buried my face in his neck as tears began to fill my eyes.

He gently lifted my chin up, so that we were face to face. "I have no right to try to talk you out of this. I think you're making a mistake and that is all I will say. Even though we aren't together, you know I love you…right?

"Yes—and I love you, too." I wanted to say more, should have said more but couldn't.

His arms wrapped around me. I felt as if my whole body was covered in those arms that I loved having around me. He hugged me so tight, like he would never let go. His lips found mine and a passionate, intense, long kiss followed. It was a kiss that said goodbye, but it also said—*remember me.*

I stood at the front window and watched him walk away. The tears began to fall freely now that I knew that he wasn't looking at me. I knew I'd done the right thing—hadn't I? Why was I second-guessing myself the second he was nice to me?

I walked up the stairs slowly, as if almost in a trance. I wasn't in the mood to watch television, so I put the radio on instead. I sat in the darkness and replayed the night over and over in my mind. I wasn't aware of anything around me until I heard a haunting song, "Babe I am leaving I must be on my way, the time is drawing near...I'll be lonely without you...I'll be missing you." I grabbed the stuffed animal that he gave me that said *I miss you*, held it in my arms, and cried.

Since Crystal had her own place now, I called her late that night. I was in tears and told her what just happened. She didn't say what I should do, just listened as good friends do.

The next day, his words kept echoing in my mind about George having a drinking problem. I quickly put in an SOS call to the girls. I would have them come over and help me sort this out.

Within an hour, tissue boxes in hand, they were at my door. I was so predictable they knew something had happened that would result in me crying. I explained the previous night's events to Liz and Leslie, as Crystal already knew. I begged for answers as to what I should do yet again.

After hours of rehashing, I realized that I couldn't let one night of Danny professing his love for me change and ruin what I had again with George. It was hard and it was eating me up inside, but I needed to not look to the past and work to look toward the future.

After we were done with boyfriend talk, Liz told me that she was going to a trade school to learn medical assisting and asked me to go also. I realized that I needed to look ahead and decided to see what the school was all about. The classes started soon, so we jumped in her car and took a ride to the school. I was going to focus on George and on my future. I found a course on dental assisting that sounded like something I might like to do.

I talked to my parents and explained what I planned. They thought it was a great idea, and with some finagling, they would come up with the deposit. I felt so anxious. I couldn't wait to go buy the uniforms and shoes. My uncle said he was going to get me a typewriter because they said I would need one for homework. It was only a six-month course but I would get a degree. Sadly, Liz's course was at a different time, so we wouldn't be able to carpool there.

I started school and loved it. My days were filled with learning and my nights I spent studying or with George. I never told him about Danny wanting to be friends again. I tried hard to continue on my path of moving forward. I did my best to keep thoughts of Danny out of my mind.

~* * * *~

A Saturday night a couple of weeks later made me question my decision once again. George's car broke down and was not worth fixing, so he had to borrow his brother's car. When George started to drink too much, I tried to point out that he had his brother's car. He wouldn't listen to me even after I kept saying over and over that he had enough. He kept saying that he went to the store today and that he was really happy about what he picked up. No matter how much I questioned him, he would not tell me what it was. The only thing he would say was that I would be really happy when I saw it and that it was for me. He was so drunk, I just wanted to go home and was tired of hearing him talk about this surprise that he wouldn't share. My gut was telling me that he had just picked up my engagement ring, but why play games like this and not say what it was? I could understand it being at a special place and time, but then he shouldn't have said anything.

"I just want to go home. I'm not feeling well, okay?" I just wanted to get away from him. I hated when he drank so much and I didn't like not knowing what he was talking about.

"I can't believe you want to ruin the rest of the night," he slurred.

"We can go out tomorrow night. I just don't feel good right now and want to go to bed. I'm not trying to ruin our night." I knew there was no sense trying to also explain how I didn't like being taunted about a surprise and not being told about it.

I knew I probably shouldn't have let him drive home, but I didn't want him on our couch either when he was in that condition. I was so angry with him, but didn't tell him. I just gave him a quick kiss goodnight and quickly got out of the car. "I will call you later if I feel better. Don't be mad," I said as I closed the car door.

I walked inside. The house was empty, my parents were out for the evening. I went into the kitchen and grabbed a bottle of soda. As I was climbing the stairs to go up to my bedroom, I heard a knock on my front door. *Oh no, please don't let it be George telling me he can't drive home.* I walked to the front window and peaked out to see who was there. My heart skipped a beat when I saw Danny.

Was it fate that Danny was at my door not five minutes after George dropped me off? Was he watching my house, waiting for me to come home?

"I hope it's okay that I came over?" Danny asked me.

"It's okay, but how did you know I was home?" I knew he had to be watching, but would he admit it?

"I was thinking about you all night. I watched for George's car," he hesitantly admitted.

"It is weird that you picked tonight to show up here. George got really drunk tonight and really pissed me off. He told me he picked up something at the store today, but wouldn't tell me what it was, just that it was for me." Why did I just tell him all that information? I instantly regretted the can of worms I knew I just opened.

"What do you think it is?" he questioned.

"I'm not sure, but he seemed really happy and excited about it."

"I don't like the sound of that. You don't think he got that ring you told me about, do you?" he hesitantly asked.

"I really don't know—I am thinking that is what it might be, though." Why? Why did I open my mouth? Deep down, I think I must have wanted Danny to say I couldn't marry

George, that he wanted to marry me. I glanced over at Danny as I awaited his thoughts.

"You can't marry him!" he snapped.

"Umm, yes I can!" I instantly got defensive. As much as I wanted this reaction from him, I also didn't think he had a say in this because he didn't want me. "If I choose to say yes, there isn't anything you can do about it, is there?" Was I baiting him to fight for me? *Oh my God, what am I doing here?*

"You can't marry him because you love me and I love you!" he exclaimed as I sensed an anger building.

His words hit me like a punch in the stomach. Of course, I loved him. He was my first boyfriend, the first person I had shared my whole soul with. I was arguing with myself in my head, as I knew I'd asked for this. *What am I going to do now?* "I've never denied that—I will always love you—but that doesn't change anything!" My temper was also beginning to build.

"You're right...I don't expect you to forgive me for what I did. You have every reason in the world to not believe what I am saying. I hurt you and I am sorry," he said in a softer tone now. "I just know you will be making a mistake...We belong together."

"You can't keep doing this to me!" I softly cried. "Just when my life starts to settle down you come here and turn me upside down again. I don't know what I am supposed to do anymore, I really don't."

"You can believe me this one last time and give us one more chance," he stated. "We belong together and you know it."

"Are you serious? You want me to go out with you again? You don't want to be with me, you just don't want me with George!"

"You know that's not true!" he argued. "Yes, I don't want you with him, but that is not why I think we should get back together. Ever since the last time we talked, all I thought about was you being with someone else and I can't handle it. I promise you this time will be different. You can't marry him. I think we should seriously think about getting engaged."

"WHAT? Are you high?" I couldn't believe what he just told me. He thought we should talk about getting engaged?

"No! I am not high. I don't want to lose you ever again," he firmly stated as he grabbed my hand and pulled me close to him.

"You gave up smoking pot? I need to know, because if you're going to be doing that then we really can't even think about getting together."

"I am not smoking anymore, I mean it," he answered.

I studied his face and saw sincerity, or what I believed it to be. I could hear my heart beating faster as I laid my head on his chest. My hair, now long and wavy, seemed to cascade upon him. I could hear every beat of his heart and every breath he was taking as I leaned against him deep in thought. I felt an instant fire ignite in my toes that traveled up through my whole body, causing me to tremble as our hearts beat together.

He gazed deep into my eyes, told me again that he loved me, as he wrapped his arms around me, and kissed me.

My whole body woke up and yearned for every touch of his hands that were all over me, and for his lips on mine, as we folded into one person, united once again.

If it was even possible, I fell more deeply in love with him after that night. After he left, I was alone with my thoughts, and reality smashed me in the side of my head. I needed to break up with George once again—and once again because of Danny. I was really afraid of how he was going to react, especially suspecting that he had paid for a ring for me.

I managed to put it off for a day, saying that I still didn't feel good, but I knew I was running out of time. An emergency call to Leslie and Liz was made. This time, when they showed up with the tissues, I didn't need them but my situation was clearly not good. No one wanted to be in my shoes; I didn't want to be in my shoes. I was floating on a cloud of happiness, yet I had to get through the worst storm in history in order to have that sunshine that would be on the flip side.

~* * * *~

"Tell me you are joking, you can't be serious." George's words of despair echoed in my head. I just told him that I was breaking up with him because of his drinking.

The tears were falling down my cheeks quickly. I did care about him, but I had to follow my heart, didn't I? I couldn't even look him in the eyes.

He reached into his pocket and pulled out a box.

A box that I knew was holding an engagement ring for me.

"I was going to give you this tonight at dinner," he softly said as tears were building in his eyes as well.

"I am so sorry. I know you don't believe me and I don't blame you one bit," I barely managed to say.

"This has to do with Danny, doesn't it? You want me to believe it is my drinking but I don't believe you!" His voice was filled with anger.

"It does have to do with your drinking! Why did you have to get so drunk the other night? If you were so happy about us getting engaged why couldn't you have shared that happiness with me, instead of with a bottle?" I just couldn't let him know that it was Danny, and I really wasn't lying, in a way.

"Just leave. I don't want to see you right now!" he yelled.

I walked away in tears. As much as I wanted to get back with Danny, I felt really bad about the pain I just caused someone who truly loved me and wanted to marry me. I told Danny that I couldn't see him that night; I needed time to myself. I had a lump in my throat that wouldn't go away. I knew I did what I needed to do, but that didn't make it any easier.

I told Danny that I had to see George one last time. I kept seeing his face standing there with the ring box in his hand, and I knew I needed to try to talk to him one last time.

A few days later, I went to see George. I wanted to make sure that he was okay and tried to explain it better. I thought if I gave him some time we could talk better. I spent all of the previous night going over in my head what to say. I just didn't want it to end the way it did.

I walked up to the door and rang the bell. I didn't tell him I would be there. I tried to call him on the phone a few times the previous week, but got no answer.

His brother opened the door and a look of hate filled his face. He just stood there glaring at me.

"Is George here?" I softly asked. I was really scared by the look on his face and my hands began to tremble.

"He didn't tell you? He sold your ring, bought a car, and left. He moved out of New York because of you!" With that, he slammed the door in my face.

What had I done? I was beyond dumbfounded at the chain of events.

I needed to see Danny. I needed him to hold me and tell me that everything would be all right. I needed to know that I didn't just make the worst decision of my life. I rang his phone once as soon as I got back home.

In seconds, he called me back.

"Please come over, I need you!" I cried.

In moments, he was walking in my front door. He found me crying on my bed. He didn't say a word but wrapped those arms I so desperately needed around me and just held me tight. He didn't question me until later about what happened to get me so upset. We decided not to talk about George and what happened after that night. We were anxious to begin our lives together, once again.

~* * * *~

Danny was true to his word. Time flew by for us and things were better than they'd ever been. He wanted to spend a lot of time with me. He called me when he said he was going to. We didn't fight all the time, and life was the way it was meant to be. I continued dental school, and we enjoyed life as the couple we were destined to be. We talked often about getting engaged soon. We even went and bought a phony ring for me to wear for the time being until we could get a real one.

The first day I walked into class with the ring, my dental schoolteacher flipped. She couldn't tell that it wasn't real, and had no reason to think differently. She was so happy for me. I was happy for me, too!

I was doing great in dental school, getting all 90s and I really enjoyed going. It was going to be really sad once we graduated and we wouldn't get to see each other every day. I wasn't even nervous about the final. I knew that I would do really great on it.

On graduation day, Danny was right there by my side cheering me on. After the ceremony, my teacher came over to us and handed us a wedding present. I was completely shocked by her act of kindness and knew I would really miss her.

At the graduation dinner dance, we shared a magical night. We slow-danced to every song that played, with our eyes locked on each other and arms holding tight. We were a couple deeply in love, for the first time in our history we were truly happy and in our minds, we were engaged.

I found a dental assisting job quite easily and was anxious to begin working. I'd never been happier than I felt right then. I had everything I wanted and was anxious to move forward.

I heard that Air Supply would be coming to a local theatre. My mom loved their songs as much as I did, so she offered to go with me and even offered to buy us the tickets. Even though Danny and I were together, there was no way he would want to go to a concert like that. I was really getting close to my mom and looked forward to a night out with just her and me.

Our seats were fantastic. Mom knew every song just like I did. It was a perfect way for her and me to enjoy some time away from the house, just us girls. Before and after the show we talked a lot about Danny and she was really happy that things were going so well for us. It was a truly perfect night.

~* * * *~

Christmas time was upon us. It felt like being in heaven when you're with someone you love. Everything seemed prettier and I couldn't wait to share the holidays together. We agreed that we were going to wait until sometime next year to really get engaged. I was still wearing my phony ring, which was just fine with me. He wanted to save up and get me whatever ring I wanted.

For Christmas, he gave me a new ankle bracelet with our initials and date on the back. We still said July 7, 1977 was our date, even though that wasn't really true. I gave him a new ID bracelet and my mom crocheted another gorgeous sweater for him, since he'd worn the first one out. We ate dinner with my family and we went to his house afterward to have desert. The phrase 'my face was lit up like a Christmas tree' came to mind, as I felt like all I could do was smile.

We decided not to go out for New Year's Eve. We just wanted to be at home together. We made love from one year into the next.

CHAPTER TEN

1984 – Age 21

"Do you have any idea just how happy I am right now?" I softly said to him. My head was resting on his chest and his arms were tightly wrapped around me. I felt so safe and secure.

"I love you," he whispered back. "I can't wait until we're married and we can be like this all the time."

"I love you, too," I responded, as I found his lips in the dark and kissed him. "It will be so nice to be able to stay together and not have to say goodbye."

I hated that he had to leave. It would've have been so nice to be able to stay wrapped in his arms all night long and wake up with him by my side, someday.

"Why don't you see if Leslie is free tomorrow night, or should I say tonight since it is so late? I'll get Dave, we'll go to dinner and a movie. Sound good?" he asked.

"Sounds good, hopefully she's free. If not, maybe Beth can go." I was truly ecstatic and beaming in every sense of the word. What a truly great start to the New Year. I just knew that this was going to be the best year of my life.

We worked during the day. Our nights were filled with quiet time relaxing at home, movies, dinners, parties, friends, and lots of laughter. We were making memories that would last a lifetime.

I never questioned nights when Danny and I didn't see each other. I felt secure in our relationship and our plans for the future together. I trusted him with every ounce of my soul.

On Valentine's Day, a huge, beautiful bouquet of roses was delivered with a note attached.

Dear Cassidy,
I love you so much!
Forever & Always,
Love Danny

I called to thank him and he told me that he was taking me out to dinner that night.

Sitting in the dimly lit restaurant, I stared at him and my heart overflowed with the love I felt for this man. I couldn't help but smile as I sat daydreaming, and forgot everything else around us.

"What is that look for?" Danny asked with a laugh.

"What look?" I asked with a giggle. "I just love you so much and I'm happy, is that a crime?"

A smile that lit up the room crossed his face. "Of course not, silly. I love you too." He reached across the table and gently caressed my hand.

~* * * *~

We talked constantly about getting married and planned our future together. I thought back to the past and how close I'd come to not having what I did right then. What if I hadn't taken that risk and not given him another chance? Where would I be then? Would I have been so close to having all my dreams fulfilled? I believed with all my heart that we were destined to be together. Last time just wasn't the time it was supposed to happen.

"What's wrong?" I asked Danny. I'd noticed something not quite the same the previous few days, but I couldn't put my finger on it. This was the first time I saw him in three days, which hadn't happened since we got back together. Every time I called, he wasn't home.

"Nothing, serious. I am just really tired. Work is busy lately. Now that the warmer weather is starting, it has been crazy. By the way, I am going to have to work quite a few nights this week, so don't be mad at me, please?"

"I've barely seen you all week." I tried to not sound angry, but I clearly was.

"I know, but there's nothing I can do. Go talk to my dad and tell him you don't want me to work. It's not like I have a choice. Do you really think I would rather work than be with you? We will go out this weekend, I promise, wherever you want to go. Just think, the more money I make, the faster we can get married."

It was hard to hide the disappointment from my voice but I tried to. "All right, but you can't expect me to be happy about it." I knew he needed to do what his dad told him, but that didn't mean I had to like it and that I didn't miss him every minute we were apart.

"Come here." He motioned for me to come closer. "I am sorry…really, but this is my job and I need you to understand that. I don't want to fight about it." He pulled me closer and in an instant, I was in his arms.

"I do understand—well, I am trying, I just miss you," I mumbled as I gazed into those blue eyes that I loved so much.

"I miss you, too! Let's go take a ride. Go grab a sweatshirt," he suggested.

"Where are we going?" A ride sounded really nice right then, to get my mind off not getting to see him much in the coming days.

"Let's go take a walk on the boardwalk," he replied.

"I like the sound of that." I loved it there. There was just something so romantic about being on the boardwalk, walking hand in hand, and hearing the ocean.

It was a beautiful spring night. Not too hot and not too cold. The sky teemed with stars and a large orange moon. It was really breezy by the water, which messed up my hair. I tried not to worry about how it looked, but clearly that was a lie, I did care.

We found a bench to sit on and talked for hours. He took my hand in his and our fingers intertwined. The sound of the ocean waves pounding the shore was mesmerizing. I daydreamed about getting engaged at a moment like this one. *How romantic it would be.* I would have loved for it to be on a beach, maybe at sunset, and to be asked if I would be his wife.

~* * * *~

I am late, oh my God no, not now. Not when life was finally going the way it was supposed to be. I just can't be pregnant, not now. I quickly picked up the phone and called Liz. "Liz you need to come over right away." I cried.

"Do not tell me that he pulled shit on you again, I will kill him!" Liz screamed.

"No, it's not that, just please come over right away."

Time seemed to stand still as I waited for her to come over with my mind reeling about what I would do. I wanted to do everything the right way. I wanted a big wedding, not a shotgun one with me being pregnant. I didn't wait all this time to have everything ruined now. Maybe I'm just stressed and not pregnant. Oh, how I prayed so hard to not be.

Liz came over and I explained what I suspected. Thank God for her and her calm reassurance that no matter, what everything would be fine.

"My parents will kill me!" My whole body was shaking by now with fear of this being a possibility. We were always careful. I'd been on the pill forever and have always been regular ever since starting them.

"You truly need to calm down. There are many reasons you could be late, don't jump to conclusions. It's only a couple days late and it can happen to anyone."

"But—you know me I'm never late like this. I am so scared." A single tear rolled down my cheek and fell onto my shirt.

"Listen, you really need to not go there. I know it's easy for me to say, but whatever happens it will be okay. You were getting married anyway, so it's truly not the end of the world."

"I want the big wedding. I don't want to be one of those pregnant brides."

"I'll get a test, but I think you should give it a few more days and just try hard to relax. You also should tell Danny…just in case you are."

~* * * *~

I didn't want to tell Danny over the phone. He was working a lot and so our time together was very scarce. I missed him terribly but there was nothing I could do about it. There were days when I didn't get to speak to him at all. I tried to be understanding and kept praying each day to find out that I wasn't pregnant. I kept hearing his words in my head that all his extra work hours would get us closer to getting married. Maybe he was saving for an engagement ring?

My phone rang once. I quickly called back.

"Hey, I am off tonight. Do you want to go to Sizzler and then see a movie at the drive in?" Danny asked.

"Definitely, that sounds good!" I was so happy to be finally spending a night with him. It wasn't really that long but every day apart seemed like a lifetime to me. I intended to try to find the courage to tell him tonight.

He was quieter than usual at dinner, but I attributed it to his long days and nights working. I decided to keep my problem a secret and not tell him tonight. I hadn't seen him much and didn't want anything to ruin the night. He already seemed not himself. At the drive-in it wasn't long before we ignored the screen and became mesmerized with each other. It was as if we couldn't get enough of each other, not wanting our lips to separate, as the time apart had clearly made us long more for each other. We didn't want the night to end, so when the movie credits were rolling, he quickly sneaked the car into another movie that was just beginning.

I wanted to be this content forever. I didn't ever want this feeling to end. I longed for the day when our nights together would end behind the same door. I found myself daydreaming more than ever about being his wife and having children, just not having a child now. It helped me get through the days and nights that I spent without him by my side.

When he kissed and hugged me goodnight, I didn't want to let go.

The next day when my phone rang once and I called him back, I was shocked to find out he was able to see me again so soon. He hadn't had two nights off in a long time. He sounded strange on the phone, or maybe it was just my imagination. All I knew was I was thrilled to be able to see him again.

When he picked me up an hour later, I began to worry as I saw a look of sadness all over his face. Little did I know everything was about to change forever.

"What's wrong? I can tell by the look on your face that something is going on," I said instantly.

"We—um—we need to talk. Let's go for a ride, okay?" He sounded clearly shaken.

"Should I be worried?" I asked as fear had completely taken over.

He didn't answer. We got in the car and he started driving. I couldn't imagine what was wrong but I felt really nervous. I kept thinking maybe he was going to have to work even more and he was afraid to tell me. He knew how much I missed him when we weren't together.

We drove to one of our usual spots by the dock. He shut the car off but left music playing softly in the background. We sat in silence for what seemed like a long time.

"You have me really scared here. What is wrong?" I didn't want to ask but I needed to know. My curiosity was in full force. I had to know what on earth had him so upset. At least I knew it wasn't that he couldn't play hockey that year. I was looking at his profile in the moonlight because it was all I could see.

"We need to break up. I am not going to be able to see you anymore." He gulped heavily.

"What? This is some sort of joke, right?" I was waiting for him to say he was kidding, or smile. "Why are you playing games with me? Everything has been so good, what the hell is going on here?" I felt as though a rug had just been pulled out from beneath me. I just didn't understand where this was coming from.

"I—I really don't know how to tell you. I have wanted to, and should have a long time ago. I just didn't want to have to let you go."

"I don't understand! What are you talking about?" Tears were beginning to fill my eyes. I was trying to hold them back but they began to trickle down my cheeks. I could tell this was really serious now and I felt so scared. Yet, I didn't want to believe this was the end. Not now when everything had been so perfect since we got back together.

"After I tell you, you are going to hate me. I don't want you to hate me. You are not going to believe that I love you."

"Tell me, dammit! I need to know." I was still thinking that we could fix it, whatever it was. I wouldn't hate him and everything would be fine.

He leaned his head forward, as he began to stare at his lap. He hesitated before finally saying, "I got someone pregnant."

There was no way that I heard what I just did, I couldn't have. How could this be? How could he have gotten someone pregnant? He cheated on me? So many questions were running through my mind, yet I couldn't find the strength to ask them. "What?" Was all I could ask, as the tears began to steadily fall from my eyes. There was no way I could tell him now that I also to might be pregnant.

"You don't know her. I have known her for a while now and I have been kind of seeing her, on and off."

"This can't be happening! Why are you doing this to me? You have been seeing someone else—why? Why?" The tears were now running like rain down my cheeks.

"I am sorry. I really didn't know how to tell you, but—there is more..." His voice softly trailed off.

"More? What else could there possibly be?"

"When her parents found out they threw her out of the house. She is living at my house now. I really hate to say this but...I am going to marry her. We are going to get married by a justice of the peace in a few weeks."

I couldn't breathe. I felt as if someone was suffocating me as his words kept playing over and over in my mind. I was in complete hysteria at that point. The kind of tears and crying where there are no words that can even make it out of your mouth. I couldn't stop. I could sense him staring at me as his hand reached over to try to comfort me.

"Home!" Was the only word I somehow managed to say as I pushed him away. I wanted to be as far away from him as I could possibly be. I just wanted to go home.

He paused and then started the car. I could sense him staring at me but I wouldn't look up. Even though we weren't that far from home the car ride seemed to take forever. I couldn't stop crying. It was really over—this was the end. After all the years I had known him, all we had shared, this was how it would end. When he pulled up in front of my house, I was opening the car door before the car stopped.

"Wait," he said. "I don't want you to go—not like this."

I glared at him through my tear-filled eyes, pausing for one last look at this man I loved more than anything. I then turned, ran into my house and slammed the door.

I plowed past my parents who were sitting on the couch in the living room, watching television. My sobs were uncontrollable. They knew instantly something really bad just happened.

"Are you okay? What's wrong?" I heard my mother's concerned voice ask as I was running up the stairs.

I barely made it to my bedroom, slammed the door closed, fell onto my bed, and cried harder than I ever have in my life. I heard my mom knocking on my door. There was no way to even try to hide my hysterics and I couldn't even talk.

"Can I come in?" my mother softly asked, as she slowly started opening my door.

I was sure she was scared. I had cried many times, but I clearly was in a condition that made her afraid for me. But I couldn't talk about it right then. I didn't want to talk about it. I just wanted the world to stop spinning, so I could get off. I wanted to die. I didn't want to face a life that he would never be in again. I knew if I tried to tell my mother what happened it would only make me cry even harder.

I managed to get the words "It's over—forever," out between the sobs.

My mom took me in her arms, didn't ask another question, and just let me cry.

I stayed in bed for days. I wasn't hungry. I wouldn't talk to anyone on the phone. My phone had rung once a couple of times but I just ignored it. If he thought I would talk to him, he was crazy. I kept replaying the other night. I didn't understand how he could do this to me. I knew we'd had many ups and downs, but we always seemed to find a way back to each other. This time we couldn't—this time there was no way to repair our relationship. My heart was shattered, in a way I never knew was even possible.

Dear Danny,

This has to be one of the hardest letters I have ever had to write in my life. For the past seven years, I thought we were holding onto something special and rare, but you have shown me that isn't true. I hope you have someone who will love you as much as me and understands you the way I do. I devoted myself to making you happy. I was always there for you through good and bad. I gave you all the love that I had to offer. I wish I could say you were always there when I needed you or when I just needed someone to hold me. I don't think I deserve this. I am the one who loves you more than anything and believes in you when no one else does. I wish to God with all my heart and soul things were different or could change. I waited so long to have you back. I hurt so much, I wish you were here to hold me! I will always love you more than you can imagine. That love will go on forever without you. My love for you is so real. I wish you all the best in everything the world has

*to offer you. I will never ever forget you and the
love you have brought into my life. Please don't
forget me. I really need to believe you will
always love me too!*

*My love to you Forever & Always. In my
heart I will always be yours, always!*
Cassidy

<u>Our Final Goodbye</u>
The flower our love was blooming on
Has withered and died away
I wish I could have believed
Our love was here to stay
The road we were on
Has come to a sudden end
You no longer will be able
To be my best friend
These last seven years
Have gone by so fast
It really hurts me
To think of us as only a past
They say the pain
Will go away
They say the tears will stop
But, it really looks like it's here to stay
How do I pretend?
That all my feelings are gone?
How can I make myself realize
That life must go on
My whole life has
Fallen apart

When here I thought
Things were just beginning to start
But, now I must
Set my love for you free
For you see
This is the way things must be
You are not free
To love me anymore
I hope you know what you are doing
I hope you are sure
Kiss me goodbye my love
Life was the best with you
Kiss me goodbye
I will go on being blue especially without
you.

When the phone rang today, I finally
decided to answer the phone. I truly needed
someone to talk to.

It was Liz she said she'd been so worried
about me.

I filled her in on what happened trying hard
to not get hysterical. I had cried far too much
these last couple days.

"What do you mean you didn't tell him?
And why didn't you answer the phone the last
couple days and tell me? I would have been
there for you!" Liz yelled at me.

"I know you would, I just needed time
alone to think."

"You need to tell him! He can't just go sleeping around and everyone else be left with the consequences of it."

"I know I should, I will if I find out I really am."

"NO! You should tell him either way, he is such a snake! If you don't, then I certainly will!"

I had no intention of calling Danny and certainly no intention of telling him there was a remote chance that I also was carrying his baby. I couldn't speak to him and he would think I was lying to try to get him back. "Let's just see what happens for now okay? Please?"

"I will drop it for today I know you have a lot going on right now, but you have to do this."

~* * * *~

I found out the next day that Liz ran into Danny at the store and gave him hell. She also told him that I was late, which I wish she hadn't but in some ways maybe it was for the best, because I knew that I couldn't call him. She must have just barely left him when my phone rang once.

I didn't want to face him and I certainly didn't want to discuss any possibility of me also being pregnant. I called him instead of ringing the phone. I wasn't going to meet him in person and truthfully, I didn't want to talk face to face. "Liz shouldn't have told you, but now you know and when I know for sure, I will let you know." I said to him in as nasty a voice as I could muster up.

"Are you playing with me? Or is this for real?"

"The fact that you even have to ask me something like that after what you have done to me—is just about as low as you could possibly go!"

"I'm sorry! There's nothing else I can say." He sounded truly concerned.

"You're right, there isn't. Don't worry about it, all right, when I know for sure I will certainly tell you!" I slammed the phone down and hung up on him.

My phone instantly rang once again, and I just ignored it.

I called the doctor and got an emergency appointment for the next day. I needed to know what was happening. Was I truly in the same situation as this girl he cheated on me with and if I was, what on earth was I going to do?

Liz came with me to the doctor, who did a blood test and an examination. Based on what she saw on the sonogram, I wasn't pregnant. She would call me tomorrow when she got the blood test back anyway, but felt that maybe I was just stressed out and that was causing me to be late. If I didn't have it by next week I would have to go back for further testing.

Three days later when my period finally arrived as I sat in tears with the worst cramps ever, I wondered if I truly wanted to be pregnant. Did I really wish that I were pregnant also, so that he maybe would have chosen to marry me instead of her? Danny had been calling every day waiting to find out and each day, I just ignored his calls. Today when he called, I told him I wasn't, that he was free to marry her without worrying about me, but deep down I think I was beginning to worry about me and where my head was. How was I going to be able to move on, yet again?

~* * * *~

"You're invited to the wedding and you are going?" I cried to my parents. "You can't be serious!" I knew my mother's love for him was like a son, but how could they go watch him marry someone else? It was supposed to be me! I didn't even wait for them to answer. I stormed up to my room and slammed the door so loud the house shook. How could my parents go to it? Did no one understand how I felt? Did no one care? I felt so alone. *Maybe I should just kill myself then they will see. I feel like everyone*

*was betraying me. What did I do to deserve
this?*

I grabbed my car keys and left the house. I
didn't want to hear any of their explanations. I
didn't know where I was going and probably
shouldn't have been driving. I found myself at
the dock. It looked so different in daylight. This
was where we said goodbye. This was where
my whole life as I knew it changed, all in one
fateful night. Air Supply's song *Here I Am* came
on the radio. I heard the words, *"just when I
thought I was over you."* I closed my eyes and
began to cry again. How was I ever going to be
over him? He was going to be someone else's
husband and a father. He was supposed to be
mine!

I went straight to my room when I got back
and would not speak to my parents at all. I
would not even let them justify their reasoning
for attending what was clearly the end of my
life. I finally called the girls, who showed up a
short time later with a box of tissues. *They truly
must be so tired of my crying by now.* Lots of
tears later and after their initial shock at hearing
what had happened wore off, we decided we
needed a girls' night. But we decided to stay
in—safer. We took a trip to the store to stock up
on lots of snacks and tried to avoid talking any
more about what was going to happen really
soon.

They tried to come up with something that
we could do the day of the wedding, so I could
be as far away as possible, but I wouldn't listen.
I didn't want to go out and as much as I loved
them, I just wanted to be alone that day.

~* * * *~

I could see the backyard from my bedroom
window. I could see people starting to arrive
and decorations hung around the yard. I knew
that it must be over by that time. They were
officially married and would be arriving at the
party soon. I didn't see my parents, but I knew
they were somewhere at that house. I didn't
know why I was sitting there torturing myself. I
could have, should have, gone out with my
friends that day and stayed away from the scene
unfolding before me. I could grab my keys,
jump in my car, and be far away from there in
seconds, but I didn't leave. I was mesmerized. I
prayed for my phone to ring and for him to tell
me that he couldn't do it. For him to tell me that
he didn't love her, that he only loved me.
Everyone would be angry at him that he skipped
out on her, and we would have to run away.

I didn't want to accept that this was really
the end. I believed with all my heart that he
really loved me and I knew that I loved him so

much more than anyone realized. But, he didn't
call or show up at my door and surprise me. The
party went on; I could hear the laughter and
music playing. I picked up one of my saddest
45s I had, placed it on the stereo, continued to
stare out my window, and cried as my world
continued to cave in around me.

> Love rolls in like the tide
> And as it rolls back out to sea
> It takes away the broken shells
> Like the part you took from me
> Again and again
> The surf smashes upon the shore
> Yet, as always
> I kept coming back for more
> As I reach out to hold you
> Only sand sifts through my fingers
> I try my best to forget you
> Yet still the feelings linger
> Waves pound against the beach
> Like my heart pounds within my chest
> That is how I knew you were someone
> Who rose above all the rest

I felt as if my life was over. I didn't know
how I was going to get over it. My heart ached
for him. I wanted to hold him in my arms again.
I wanted to hear his voice. I missed everything.
I just wanted him back. I was finding it hard to
work and even though my friends kept trying to

get me to go out, I didn't want to. I felt as if part of me died and I didn't know how to move on. I didn't know if I even wanted to. I moved through my days and nights in a complete fog.

I avoided places where I might run into him. It worked for a while until fate decided to step in and knock me right back down. It was October 2nd and it was the first time I was face to face with him since that fateful day we said goodbye. It was so hard to see him. He looked like he was happy, but I also believed that he felt the same as me somehow. He told me that the baby was due the following month. I was still finding that a hard one to accept. He looked so different. He had a beard and mustache. He told me that he would call me soon, and I felt in my heart that somehow, someway, someday, I would have him back in my life.

My short conversation with Danny that shouldn't have given me any hope for a future did just that. Even though I knew he was married and about to have a baby, I would not believe that it was the end forever,—it just couldn't be.

I started to live again. I finally agreed to go out with friends and for the first time in a very long time, I found myself smiling.

Weeks later, Danny called and he told me that she had the baby and it was a girl. I couldn't believe he was now a dad. I felt as if someone has just grabbed my heart and was squeezing it really tight.

I barely listened to what he was saying, until his next words shocked me out of my daze: "I really miss you. It's so hard not seeing you and talking to you," he said.

"I really miss you too! You have no idea what it has been like for me. I think about you all the time. It is so hard to believe that you are married and have a baby." My thoughts were screaming that this was just not fair. That should be me with him!

"You are probably going to say no, but...I am going to say I am going Christmas shopping tonight. I...would really like you to find a way to see me. We haven't been able to really talk in a long time," he said softly.

He wanted to see me? He missed me? Those were magical words to my broken heart. I knew it was wrong. I knew there was no way I should agree to see him. Yet—I found myself pondering the notion and just wanting one more day with him. "You really think this is a good idea? How? You can't just come pick me up. My parents will freak out!" I couldn't believe I was even thinking about doing it.

Since Crystal had her own apartment, I asked her if I could meet him at her place. It was the only place that would be safe. I hated to ask her, but it was the only place we could meet unnoticed. After a long conversation explaining the importance of this, she agreed. I could only imagine what was going through her mind, though. As one of my best friends, she also understood it was something I felt I must do.

I arrived early at her apartment and sat trying to be patient, waiting for him to arrive. My heart was racing. I couldn't wait to see him.

He finally arrived after what seemed like a lifetime of sitting and waiting. I just couldn't believe my eyes! He was here with me. There was awkward silence between us at first, so we began to make small talk.

Crystal decided to go out and get us all ice cream. I think she was just trying to give us some time alone.

I glanced over at Danny and felt an instant tug at my heart. There were no words for the emotions that stirred every time I saw his face or heard his voice. Our eyes locked and words weren't even necessary to speak.

I told him all about my new job as an oral surgery assistant/receptionist. My new boss was great and seemed to love the work I was doing. I told him that on Wednesdays I worked in the office alone. I just had to sit and answer the phones. If any major emergencies came up, I had to call the doctor and he would come in.

Time went too fast and before I knew it, he said he needed to leave. Even though stores were open late for Christmas shopping, he didn't want her to get suspicious. It was so nice being able to sit near him and just talk. There was so much more to tell him and so much, I wanted to know. I didn't want to say goodbye and I sensed he didn't either, yet that's what we had to do. I walked him to the door and the awkward silence was back.

He pulled me into his arms and hugged me tight.

I didn't want him to let go.

When he pulled away, our eyes met. "I love you," he softly said, as he gave me a kiss.

"I love you, too." I hated that! We shouldn't have had to say goodbye. I was the one he should have been going home to, not her. I didn't tell him what I was thinking. There was no point.

"I will call you when I can." With that, he was gone.

An emptiness filled me. I was left alone to deal with all the emotions running through my mind once again. It was my own fault, but I just loved him so much. As wrong as it was, I did not enjoy life when he wasn't in it.

I was so depressed after seeing Danny. I prayed each day for the phone to ring and to hear that he had arranged for us to see each other again. I put on a good show, going about my days as normally as I could. Nights, I laid awake crying for the love that I missed so terribly. I felt as though I was in a fog so thick, I couldn't see anything around me. Days blended together and nights left my heart yearning for what I couldn't have.

I began to believe that our one night together was just that, one night and there might not be another. I managed to get through the holidays, but every song I heard and everywhere I went reminded me of our last Christmas. We were together dreaming and planning for a future. We were so happy and time seemed to be magical. I believed that by now, a ring would have been placed on my finger and we would begin plans for a wedding. I wondered if he was thinking of me and missing what we had together. Did he miss me like I missed him?

CHAPTER ELEVEN

1985 – Age 22

I knew my life had to go on. I also knew that it wasn't going to be easy, but I could no longer continue to sit around and wait for calls that wouldn't come. I picked up my shattered self and began to live.

Leslie, Liz, and Crystal were so happy to hear that I had finally come to my senses.

The girls and I went to a club the first chance we could and as luck would have it, I ran into Kyle and his friends. He was on his way out but told me that he was bartending at a place called Gadgets. He asked me to stop there the following night to see him while he was working. It'd been a long time since I'd seen him. I wondered if there still might be a chance for us. I quickly told the girls, who were thrilled and agreed to go with me.

I took extra care getting ready the next night, as I didn't know what to expect, and I wanted to look really good. I wanted Kyle to want me back. It was too cold to wear a mini-skirt, so I settled for my new Jordache jeans from Christmas and a nice shirt.

Crystal offered to drive. We had come up with a plan to take turns driving. When she drove, I could drink and vice versa. That way we didn't ever drive drunk. We found the place without any problems and quickly fell in love. There was a large dance floor and lots of nice looking guys. We made our way to the bar.

When Kyle noticed me, a huge smile filled his face. He told me that he was happy that I showed up and hoped I could hang out late, so maybe we could talk later. My friends ordered their drinks and then quickly left, so I could talk to Kyle alone. We caught up on boring chat about what we'd been doing.

He was surprised to hear that I had graduated dental assistant school and told me that he was happy for me. He didn't ask if I was seeing anyone, but I was hoping he'd asked me here to get back together. It was so busy that it was really hard to talk while he was working and the loud music was blasting.

I told him I would stay late, so we could talk later. He handed me a Long Island Iced Tea and a melon ball shot. I put money on the bar but he didn't take it.

I told him I would be back in a while and went to find where my friends had disappeared to. I scanned the dance floor and saw Leslie dancing with a really nice looking guy. I found Crystal and Liz sitting at a table.

The minute I sat down, they started asking me questions about Kyle and if we were going to get back together. I knew they just wanted to see me back to my old self and over Danny finally. I told them it was too hard to talk while he was working and that I was going to talk to him later when it died down a bit. Hopefully, if all went well, he would drive me home.

It was so much fun dancing. It'd been so long. I found myself smiling and laughing for the first time in a really long time. A nice looking guy asked me to dance, which I happily accepted, and I danced with him until my feet began to hurt. I didn't exchange numbers or anything with the guy but he told me he would look for me later. I was dying of thirst, so I made my way back to the bar where Kyle was. I didn't have to wait long before he noticed me standing there.

"Can you do me a favor? Can you please not pick up guys in front of me?" he asked.

It only took a second to register that he was jealous and didn't like seeing me with someone else. That was a really good sign. "I was only dancing," I laughingly told him. "I didn't even exchange numbers with the guy."

"Well…I don't like seeing you with someone else, okay?" he stated.

"Okay," I answered hesitantly. I was beyond shocked to find out he still cared.

When I got back to the table and told the girls, they all said the same thing—that he still loved me and they thought we would get back together. I would know better later what the story was. I just danced the rest of the night away until my feet were on fire and I couldn't any more. It was decided that I would get a ride from Kyle and the girls left not long before the place was closing.

We sat in the car for a long time, talking. It was nice to catch up on what we'd both been doing. He couldn't believe what happened with Danny, although he was probably happy that there wouldn't be an issue about me getting back with him. He seemed to genuinely feel bad for me and the pain I went through. We decided that we weren't going to rush things. He was just getting over a recent break up and wanted to stay single for a while, so we agreed that we would just take things slow. I didn't want to hurt him. I knew that as much fun as the night had been, and how happy I was to have made him jealous, deep down my heart was still missing Danny.

Kyle said when he had a weekend night off, he would take me out to dinner and we could talk more then. In the meantime, he told me to come visit him at work whenever I could.

~* * * *~

When the phone rang on January 30th at work, I was fully expecting a patient when I heard his voice, that familiar voice that turned all my common senses to mush.

"Hey, it's me. I am outside in the parking lot, is anybody there? Can I come in?" he asked.

"No one is here," I replied, as my mind began to reel in a million different directions. Since I was alone, I didn't have to wear a uniform, so I quickly glanced at my choice of clothing. Not that I could do anything about it at that point since he was already there.

"Meet me at the door," he said.

I rushed to the door and opened it.

There he was, looking as good as ever.

All it took was seeing him or hearing his voice to instantly remind me just how very much I missed him.

"How are you doing?" he asked. "It is risky for me to stay here too long, but I just had to stop by when I saw your car in the parking lot. I remember you saying Wednesdays you worked alone. I was hoping we could make plans to get together again soon."

"I'm doing all right. How are things going for you?" I truly didn't know what to say.

"Things are okay, I guess. I'm working a lot." He hesitated and then asked, "Are you going out with anyone now?

"Not really, I saw Kyle recently, but we're taking it slow." Why was he asking me that? Could he possibly be thinking of leaving her and coming back to me?

"So…do you think maybe we could meet at Crystal's again one night?" he asked me. "I'm going to be working nights soon, so I can say that I'm working."

I so wanted to see him and wanted nothing more than to feel his arms wrapped around me one more time. "I don't think that will be a problem. Just let me know when, so I can ask Crystal and make the arrangements."

"I hate to run but I don't want to get caught here. I wish I could stay…I love you!" he said as he turned towards me, gave me a quick kiss on the lips, and left.

I didn't feel guilty, although I knew that I probably should. It still seemed so unreal to me. I didn't think I would ever get used to the fact that he was married, had a baby now, and wasn't mine. I didn't cry. If our little meetings were all I could have, I would accept that. It was better than never getting to see him again or never talking to him. I didn't tell anyone that he came by and I would wait until I knew when he could get away to ask Crystal if we could meet at her apartment again. I knew my friends would tell me I was crazy and that I should just stay with Kyle, who was free.

~* * * *~

The girls and I went back to Gadgets, so I could see Kyle. It was close to my birthday, so he decided he was going to get me drunk. Drinking seemed like a good idea, helped me to forget about Danny, Kyle, and everyone else for the moment. Dancing drunk did not work too well when it started to make me dizzy. We decided to leave earlier than we did on most of our weekend nights out. I wasn't waiting until he got off that night. I tried to walk over to the bar to tell him I was leaving, but instead stumbled and almost fell.

Crystal was hysterical, laughing at me. I could barely walk by then. Liz drove that night, so Crystal was able to drink too. I thought we were both driving Liz crazy being drunk when she was sober. Leslie stayed home that night since she wasn't feeling well.

Kyle came out from behind the bar and kissed me goodbye. He told me to be careful, to call him the next day, and if I heard him correctly, I thought he said he wanted to go out again. I would have to figure out what on earth he said when I called.

When we pulled up in front of my house, everything was spinning. I opened the car door, but didn't move yet.

I heard Liz saying, "We are at your house. You can get out of the car now."

Did I sense attitude? I stood up finally.

Crystal was cracking up and laughing again as she tried to get from the back seat to the front...it wasn't as easy a task as it should have been.

I began to laugh too, as I finally made my way toward my front door, when BOOM. Yes, that was me. Seems there was ice on the ground from the previous day's little snow, which I didn't see and it caused me to fall. I sat on the ground, laughing hysterically. I could hear Liz and Crystal both cracking up too. I managed to get up. I thought I was hurt, but knew I would find out the next day when the world stopped spinning. I made my way up to my bed and passed out.

When I woke the next day, I found that my knees were bruised and cut, as were my elbows. I also vaguely remembered Kyle telling me, or at least I thought he told me, that he wanted to go out with me again. I tried to call him but got his machine. I decided not to leave a message. I thought I wanted to go out with him again, but I also didn't want to cheat on him and I was supposed to see Danny sometime soon. Not that I thought Danny and I would do more than talk.

At least, we hadn't so far, but I didn't want to risk hurting Kyle.

~* * * *~

A friend of my family worked at a travel agency and told me she had a great deal that I should take advantage of. Getting away sounded like a great idea. It was the Bahamas and everything was included in the price. Leslie and Liz weren't able to get off work but Crystal was able to work something out.

I ran into Danny on my way to get my travelers' checks. He wanted me to meet him at Chapter Two, which was a bar in our town. He wanted me to go there the following night at 2:00 a.m. when he got off work. I told him I was going away for a few days with Crystal that we got a really good deal and I really didn't think I would be able to meet him. I really wanted to see him and saying that I couldn't was hard. He seemed disappointed but I had a lot to do to get ready to go away. He looked miserable that day. I wondered if things were not going well for him and his married life. I told him that when I returned, we would figure something out. We couldn't talk long as he had to get back to work.

Kyle called me to see how I was doing. I told him that I was getting away for a few days.

He said he would take us to the airport. I didn't ask him about what he might or might not have said to me the other night. Right then, I just wanted to get away and not worry about anything.

Crystal and I had a great time on our vacation. There was a casino and a dance club right in our hotel. Our days were spent laying in the sun, tanning. Nights we started at the casino until we began to lose too much, and then danced the night away in the club. The trip went way too fast and before we knew it, we were heading back home. It was so nice to not think about the mess that my life was in for at least a few days.

The first Wednesday I was back at work, Danny showed up at the door. He told me about ten times that he loved me. He told me that on July 7th he was going to find a way to get out and wanted us to go someplace special, so we could be together. There was a nice hotel called the Commack Motor Inn. It was far enough away that it would be safe to go there. He just needed to figure out how we were going to do it. I knew it was so wrong to even contemplate, but when I was with him, there was just no way to say no.

July 7th was such a magical day to both of us. It marked a date in our history when life was so simple. Love was new and pure for us. We never would have dreamed that we would wind up in the position we were in now.

He didn't stay long because he didn't want to risk being seen. I spent the rest of the day at work dreaming about what it would be like to be lying next to him and wrapped in his arms again, even if only for a short time.

The week before the 7th, I thought Danny would stop by work to let me know what he was able to arrange, but he didn't show up. I began to think he had had second thoughts. I wanted to be mad but I couldn't be. I was disappointed that maybe we wouldn't get to share an evening together. Talking at my job for the short time we did was hard. Being able to really spend hours together again, would have been nice.

~* * * *~

One day, an invitation arrived in the mail for David's wedding. He met a girl he deeply loved and had never been happier. Danny's dad told my parents that they were thinking of renting a bus to take us, since it wasn't going to be at a place close by. That way, we could all have a good time and no one would have to worry about driving. This would be the first time that I would have to be in the same place with Danny and his wife. I would never get used to saying those words. I was going to ask Kyle to go with me. There was no way that I was attending that alone, and have to see them together the whole night. Also, I would never miss David's wedding. He had been a good friend to me since day one. He never could understand how his brother could continue to hurt me.

It seemed like just yesterday I was moving into my house and meeting them both. Now, they would both had wives and families. I knew I shouldn't dwell on that, but I did. I was the one who was supposed to be with Danny and be a part of this family of theirs. I began to think that I would never get married.

July 7th came and went. He didn't even call and I began to think that maybe he had realized that seeing me really wasn't the right thing to do. I really believed he was at least going to call me that day even if he wasn't able to see me.

I ran into David at the store a couple days later and he was anxious about his upcoming wedding. I was so happy for him but I felt a tug in my heart again, wishing I was the one married to Danny.

"Have you heard the news?" David asked me.

"What news?" Instantly, I was deep down hoping to hear that maybe Danny left his wife. I knew I was a horrible person to even think that.

"My dad booked the party bus for the wedding, so that way everyone can drink and not have to worry," he said.

My heart stopped for a second. In my mind, I heard 'Danny left Wanda.' It wasn't what he really said. I realized he just told me something completely unrelated to Danny. I tried hard to hide my inner feelings. No one knew that we had even seen each other, not even his brother, so I couldn't express what I really felt. "That's really great," I stated as convincingly as I possibly could as I continued to grasp reality.

"You still love him, don't you?" David asked in a voice of someone who'd known the strange on-again and off-again relationship Danny and I shared for so many years. Deep down, I was sure even he thought that we would wind up married.

I hesitated before answering. There was no sense lying to him, "Yes—I still love him. I think I always will in some ways. Your wedding will be the first time I'll see them together."

"I'm sorry. I love him, he is my brother, but I really thought you two would've wound up together one day. But you will have a great time at the wedding, I know you will." I think he saw the pain that probably showed on my face. "Let's talk about something else, okay? Are you going to bring someone to my wedding? I still can't believe how close it is. I have never been happier than I am right now." He was completely beaming as he talked about marrying the love of his life.

"Yes, I'm going to ask Kyle to go with me. We have been seeing each other again. Nothing serious as of yet, but I think he will go with me."

"Kyle seems nice. Maybe it will work out for you with him," he stated.

"I hope so…I really do," I said, as reality of my life as a single woman hit me right in the heart.

David continued to tell me about the wedding plans until he realized the time and needed to get back to work.

Everything was starting to finally make sense to me. I missed Danny terribly but I had to truly face a reality that my heart just didn't want to face. He had moved on and was married. Even if he did love me like he said, it didn't change the reality. We would not have a future together. He wasn't going to leave her and come running back to me. I had to move on and not keep thinking in the back of my mind that we still had any hope for a future together.

It seemed so hard to look forward to seeing one of my best friends getting married and yet at the same time, I kept dreading having to face Danny with his wife together for the first time.

There wasn't much time to dwell on Danny and what should have been. When I arrived back at my house, I found my front door open.

My mom's car wasn't there, so panic instantly filled me; something wasn't right. If my mom were home, her car would have been here. I began to think someone had broken into my house. I ran next door to my neighbor, told her what I thought was going on and we quickly called the police.

My mom worked for the local police department. She was the chief of police's secretary. She'd started working there part time and was moved to full time. Everyone loved my mom, so when they got this call they arrived quickly.

Seemed like just seconds later my dead-end street was blocked off. I thought every police car had arrived. I'd never seen so many cops. They began jumping fences and went into every yard on my street. I saw them draw their guns as they began to enter my house. My heart was racing. I had never been so scared in my life.

Time seemed to stand still as I waited to see them come out of the house with whoever was in there. I stood at my neighbor's front door, so I had a perfect view of my house. When they finally came outside, I heard laughter. Everyone was smiling and laughing. I didn't understand what was happening. I saw one of the police officers wave for me to go over to him. I hesitated, still afraid to go.

"Go inside, I think you will be in for a big surprise," he said to me.

I walked slowly into my house and there in my living room was my mother, whose face was the shade of a red apple.

"Wait—you weren't supposed to be home. Your car isn't here."

"Your dad dropped me off and took my car to the gas station. I got off early. I guess I forgot to tell you I was coming home early."

"I'm sorry," I said as I glanced around my house that was completely filled with police and thought about what my street looked like.

"I don't think I will be living this down anytime soon. I was in the bathroom with the door open when they came up the stairs with their guns drawn," Mom said, laughing.

I was trying so hard not to laugh, but the thought of what just happened overruled the chaos I had just created. I felt really bad but everyone was laughing, even my mom. I knew I did the right thing, not knowing that someone was home.

I called Kyle to tell him what happened and asked him about going to the wedding with me, which he agreed to do without any hesitation. I knew that I needed to face reality once and for all. I needed to move on with my life. I couldn't keep living in the past. I hoped I could find the strength that I needed. But no matter how hard I tried, my mind wouldn't stop thinking of Danny and missing him.

CHAPTER TWELVE

September 15th

It was David's wedding day. I'd been dreading this day and looking forward to it at the same time. My stomach was doing flip-flops, anticipating having to face Danny and Wanda together for the first time. It was going to be so hard. I knew I had to be really strong and I needed to make it through the day. At the same time, I was looking forward to seeing David get married. I knew how important it was to him.

My parents were also attending and I believed having them by my side would also help me get through the day.

The bus was such a great way to go for everyone. The ride went quickly. The church ceremony was uneventful. There were so many people attending I didn't see Danny and focused on watching the wedding. We took the bus to the hall after the ceremony. I tried really hard to keep my mind off having to see Danny. Since Kyle and I were more good friends than anything else at that point, he knew my feelings about today. We talked about it for a long time one night. I didn't want to be deceitful. I just couldn't hurt him; he didn't deserve that. He wasn't looking to be serious and we had come to an understanding. As friends, we didn't need to pretend to be something we weren't. Maybe someday that would change for us, but for now, it was what worked. There were no hard feelings and our time together was much more enjoyable without the pressures.

As we walked off the bus at the hall, my heart began to race. I had no idea if Danny and Wanda were already inside.

Kyle sensed my hesitation and grabbed my hand. Our eyes locked and no words were spoken between us.

I swiftly glanced around the room, wondering where they were. I didn't see them and was finally able to let out the breath that I'd been holding.

We found our table and quickly sat down. Kyle offered to go get us some drinks, which I happily agreed to.

"How are you doing?" my mom asked as she took a seat next to me.

"I'm hanging in there. I don't see them yet, thank God." But I continually scanned the room, awaiting the impending moment.

"I know this is really a hard day for you, but don't let that get in your way of enjoying today," she urged.

Then it happened. My eyes were drawn to them as if they were a magnet with a force so strong I was pulled toward them without even wanting to be. I looked across the room and there he was, staring at me. For a moment in time, nothing else in the room existed, and everything became silent. All I saw was him and those eyes that would forever melt me. There were no other people. No one was talking and the music had disappeared. I didn't know whether to smile or look away. I was frozen. I continued to stare at him as my eyes filled with tears that I managed to somehow freeze. Even from across the room I could see the pain on his face, too.

"Here you go," Kyle said, as he sat down next to me and handed me my drink.

Then just like that—the moment was gone and the music was playing. Everyone was talking, laughing, and dancing.

"Thank you," I managed to say, as I gazed around as if I'd just woken up. Was I dreaming? I saw that Danny was gone and the place where he'd been standing was empty—just like me. *I won't do this,* I promised myself. But it was just so much harder than I ever imagined it would be. To have him there and not be able to talk to him, not be able to touch him or hold him, hurt me beyond belief.

I forced myself back to my reality, to my world without him. I had to focus on Kyle. He convinced me to dance. We danced until we were exhausted and thirsty. He went off to get us some new drinks as I headed back to our table.

I was left alone. I started to scan the room, when I finally saw her. Even though no one told me it was her, I just knew it was. I had imagined this moment for so long, but nothing could really prepare me enough. I refused to see pictures from the wedding, I just couldn't. Now, there she was. In my eyes, she had what was supposed to be mine. She had the life I'd been dreaming of and the man I still loved. Even though I knew he was just as much to blame, my anger was aimed at her. She took my place in that family. I saw her talking to Danny's mom and I found myself staring at her every move. I tried to look away, but found that I couldn't. The saying 'if looks could kill' came to mind. I had envisioned her as being unattractive, yet she was anything but. Her blonde, flattering, short hairstyle complimented her petite body in a stunning dress. She was pretty; why did she have to be pretty? I continued to stare, knowing full well I shouldn't. She must have sensed me staring because in a split second, she was staring at me, too. We didn't need to speak, our eyes glaring at each other told the whole story. I don't know how much time passed before Danny walked up to her and broke our contest.

He gave me a look, which clearly had a smile within it, as he took her attention away from me.

Kyle returned with our drinks and I returned my attention to him. It was very hard to not keep looking over at Danny and Wanda and to not watch their every move.

"You do know that he has been staring at you the whole night, don't you?" Kyle asked me.

"No, I didn't know that, he is with his wife."

"Well, that doesn't seem to be stopping him," he said in an angered tone.

"Do I sense jealously from the one who wanted to stay non-committed?" I asked him with a smile. We both had agreed on not being committed, but I sensed something was changing.

Just as he was about to answer, a slow song began to play, *Cherish* by Kool and the Gang. Kyle grabbed my hand and pulled me onto the dance floor once again. We found a place on the floor as he pulled me closely to him and wrapped his arms around me. I found myself looking at him as if I was seeing him for the first time. I knew I hadn't been fair to him at times, but he also had not wanted to be committed to me. I decided that I needed to live for today. I couldn't keep doing the rollercoaster of emotions with Danny. Maybe I was meant to be with Kyle. We'd been going back and forth almost as long as Danny and I had been. If I could just get Danny out of my mind once permanently, Kyle and I just might have a chance at a future.

The night went by quickly and I spent the rest of the evening by Kyle's side, dancing and talking. I didn't search the room looking for Danny or Wanda. I did over-hear at the bar on one of the trips for a drink that they were fighting. I didn't know what it was about, but I could only imagine, it had something to do with me. As the last song played, I realized I had made it through another hard day and night. I also knew that without Kyle there and his support, it would have been so much harder, if not impossible.

As we started our goodbyes and we wished David and Debbie the best, I saw Danny one last time, staring at me. I glanced over at him, but this time I didn't smile; I just turned away. We gathered all our stuff and headed to the bus that would take us back home.

Kyle didn't say much on the bus ride and neither did I. There was a lot to process from the night. I believed that things would finally be better and maybe Kyle and I both had learned that our feelings for each other just might be more than the friends we pretended to be.

I talked to Kyle a couple of days after the wedding and even though he clearly admitted he was jealous, we mutually agreed that we weren't going to rush into anything just yet. We would still go out occasionally and I would go visit him with my friends, but that was all it would be for now.

It was two months later while at work, when Danny showed up at my job. My heart still fluttered when I saw him, and that yearning pain to be with him still overcame me. I managed to hide it as best I could. I knew I couldn't keep doing that anymore. Danny told me that he and Wanda got into a huge fight at the wedding. It lasted for days after, due to his excessive staring at me the whole time. He told me that seeing me with Kyle bothered him so much, but he knew that he had no right to be upset about it.

The reality of our situation began to truly weigh heavy on us. What were we doing? Nothing good would come of this, and never knowing when we might get to see each other again was just too painful. He didn't stay too long; I think reality had hit us both. We didn't make plans to see each other again. That day felt like we were finally saying the goodbye we should have said a long time ago.

I wanted to cry but no tears seemed to be left. I felt alone and so empty. I wished so much to be able to go back in time and fix things, but we just weren't meant to be and the sooner I could accept that the sooner, maybe, I could have a real life and love again.

I was an empty shell, going through the motions. I worked and went out with my friends or with Kyle. We still hadn't made a true commitment to each other. I learned how to smile and laugh again, although on the inside my heart was still in pieces and they just hadn't moved back into the right places. No one knew the pain I felt inside me, and nothing would ever be the same.

CHAPTER THIRTEEN

1986 – Age 23

The holidays came and went and I was able to put on a good show. We were now into a new year in which I had vowed I would find true love and happiness. I hadn't seen or talked to Danny since November. I knew in my heart it was for the best, but I still found myself thinking of him and wondering what he was doing. I wondered, *does he think of me too?*

Days and nights all blended together. Time showed no mercy. I did everything I could to find happiness. I began to wonder if there really was such a thing, and did it even exist for me anymore. I went to clubs and met some nice guys. I even dated a couple of them, only to find that they didn't make my heart flutter or touch my soul the way I longed for.

Kyle and I tried once again to make our relationship work, only to find that he still didn't like being in a committed relationship. That shouldn't have come as a surprise to me, yet somehow it did. I kept telling myself I had known him only a year less than Danny. If Danny wasn't my forever love, maybe Kyle was the destiny that I really didn't give a fair chance to. So, I opened my heart once again, only to find it broken. Maybe he didn't want to commit to me, because he knew I still loved Danny. If so, I guess I couldn't blame him.

Halloween came and my cousin Debbie and I decided we were going to stay local that night. Debbie and I had been hanging out since we were little and I lived at my grandmother's. We lost touch for a bit because of school, but now that we were older and drove, we could see each other whenever we wanted. Debbie was a couple years younger than me.

We decided to go to a bar called Copperwaites. We hadn't gone to this place too many times, but usually when we did it had a nice crowd.

Debbie and I went to the bar to get some drinks. Two drunken, really grungy-looking guys kept staring at us.

"Hey beautiful," one of them said to Debbie.

I hastily turned away, trying to hide my laughter. Debbie was beautiful—they did get that part right—but we were not about to hang out with drunken guys. She had gorgeous, long, light-brown hair and ocean-blue eyes. Guys always turned to watch her.

Across the room, I saw a guy in a policeman's uniform. I couldn't stop staring at him. He had light brown hair with dark brown eyes and a body to die for. He was strikingly gorgeous, the type of guy you can't stop staring out. "Check out the guy in the police costume over by the jukebox."

"He is really nice looking!" Debbie said. "His friend isn't all that bad either."

We must have stared at him for an hour, then the friend of the one I liked came over and started talking to us. I didn't notice where the other one had disappeared to, but I was hoping he would come over too.

"Hi, my name is Ryan," he said more to my cousin than to me,

I was thankful he only looked at her, as I really liked his friend.

"Hi!" Debbie responded, and her face lit up.

"My friend Mike and I would like to buy you girls a drink," he said. "He should be right back. He had to run to his car for a minute. What are you two drinking?"

Instantly, I was watching the door, waiting for Mike to walk back in. I was praying that he would like me as much as I found myself liking him. "I'll take a Long Island Iced Tea," I spoke up.

"I'll take a Screwdriver," Debbie told him.

"Okay, I'll be right back and by then, Mike should be back." Ryan smiled and then walked away toward the bar.

"Oh my god, I can't believe we actually met the guys we picked out," Debbie said, laughing.

"I just hope Mike likes me; he is so good looking!"

"Ryan is pretty good looking too! How cool would it be to date friends?" Debbie replied.

"That would be way too cool. Let's hope this works out for both of us," I said as my eyes stayed glued to the door.

Then he was there, walking toward me with a smile that warmed my body that had grown to be so cold.

"Hey! I'm Mike! What are your names?"

"I am Cassidy and this is my cousin Debbie," I said, hoping I didn't sound as overly anxious and flustered as I felt.

"I know it sounds like a line, but do you come here often?" Mike laughed.

"Yes, it sounds like a line," I replied and laughed with him. "We really haven't been here too many times."

"Do you live close to here?" Mike asked me.

"I live in the next town but we usually go to places where we can dance, like Gadgets," I told him as I prayed that he liked to dance too.

"I live only a few blocks away from here. What do you do?" Mike asked.

"I am an oral surgery assistant. What do you do, Mike?"

"Well, I really am a police officer. Even though this is a Halloween costume, I'm a city policeman and fireman."

"My mom works for the Police Department. She's the chief of police's secretary," I quickly stated.

"Well Cassidy, looks like we were meant to meet!" He smiled.

"It certainly looks that way to me, too." I smiled back at him.

I scanned the bar and saw Debbie and Ryan talking in a booth nearby. She looked happy and so did he, so I was glad that we both seemed to have met nice guys for a change.

The rest of the night flew by so quickly. Mike and I didn't seem to run out of conversation and also seemed to have a lot in common. When it was time to leave, they walked us to our car.

"Silly question and I guess I should have asked earlier, but can I have your number?" Mike asked.

"Of course, you can."

We exchanged numbers and said our goodbyes. He didn't try to kiss me, nor did Ryan try to kiss Debbie. As we drove home we both couldn't get over that this was the first time we actually met what we believed to be decent guys.

Mike called me two days later. We talked on the phone for a couple of hours. He had to work that night, so he told me he would try to call me back if he could later.

He did call me back and asked me to go out with him the following night. He couldn't talk long since he was at work, but at least he wanted to go out. He told me to pick a movie that I would like to see and look up the times. He would call me during the day to set up what time he would pick me up.

I decided that we would go see *Stand by Me*. The movie was scheduled to start at 8:00, so he picked me up at 7:30. It was playing at a theatre not far away, so we had plenty of time to get there. After the movie, we went to the Time Piece Café. It's a really nice wine and cheese place, very quiet, and a perfect place to really talk. We talked for hours. We talked about everything. He told me that most girls were not looking for a commitment. That was news to me. I completely thought that it was the other way around, especially after Kyle. He referred to me as his girlfriend. I was on cloud nine. When we got back to my house after the café, we sat in his car and talked until three in the morning. I didn't even know how we found so much to talk about, but we never seemed to run out of conversation. That night, he kissed me for the first time. It was a great kiss goodnight and a perfect way to end a perfect date.

Things seemed to be so simple with Mike. I felt like I'd known him so much longer. I was trying to take things slow, but—it was so hard when for the first time in so long, life seemed perfect.

He picked me up again one day and we went to a restaurant named Gillie's to watch the Islander hockey game. We left early since I had to work early the next day, but we wound up sitting in the car again in front of my house, talking until after three a.m.

The next day unfortunately, we couldn't see each other but we did talk on the phone for hours. He told me that he had never talked so much as he'd done with me the previous few days. He told me also that he bought us tickets to Saturday night's hockey game. He even wanted to meet my parents when he picked me up. I thought I was dreaming. I found myself actually looking forward to Christmas for the first time in years. I tried to not think ahead and dream, but he just seemed perfect.

Meeting my parents went so well and they seemed to really like him. My mom had no problems talking to him since she worked in a police station. My dad even seemed to get along well with him.

We spent endless time together, days and nights sitting sometimes three hours in the car, just talking and sharing everything we loved and hated. He even opened up with me and told me that his mom was dying of cancer. I could feel his pain and cried along with him.

We had begun to count our hours of talking. We were up to 55 hours. It started as a joke but we continued to count.

One night he picked me up and we went Christmas shopping at the mall. Then we went back to my house and watched *Gremlins*. I rested my head on his shoulder and all felt right with the world. I could have fallen asleep, I was so comfortable. He didn't leave until two in the morning and we hugged that night for the first time. I never believed that I could feel the security that I felt having his arms wrapped around me.

Laying on my bed after he left, I didn't know why, but I thought of Danny. How I wished that I had with him what I had with Mike. I wondered what he was doing and if I ever even crossed his mind any more. But I found that even though once in a while I thought of Danny, those times were getting farther and farther apart. My life had finally moved on and I realized that I could have happiness and love again. A piece of me would never forget Danny or what I shared with him, but I had wasted too much time not allowing myself to truly live.

Debbie and Ryan had been getting along really well, too. It was like we were destined to find them that night. The four of us went out at least once a week and I couldn't remember laughing so hard in such a long time.

One night we went to the Time Piece Café again. We sat for hours talking about our feelings on marriage and how neither of us believed in divorce. How could that be? How, after such a short time, were we even having conversations like that? He was everything I always wanted and more. I believed someday, he would make a great husband and father.

Mike started midnight shifts for the following two weeks, so it would be harder to see each other for a while, but I wasn't worried. We would talk as much as we possibly could. I believed I had found Mr. Right and someday…I was going to marry him.

~* * * *~

Mike was finally off the midnight shifts and I could see him! It seemed like forever since I had. Even though we talked every day, sometimes for hours at a time, I wanted to see him. We went to Copperwaites. Ryan and Debbie met us there.

Ryan and Debbie had a table already, so I sat down and Ryan got up and went to the bar with Mike.

"Cas, he loves you, holy shit, I can see it in his face!" Debbie shouted at me, in a nice way. "I wish Ryan was as gaga over me as Mike clearly is over you!"

"I can't believe it, I really can't! We talk for hours and hours. We seem to believe in the same things, have the same dreams."

"Well, I am so jealous! You are going to marry him. Ryan told me even he has noticed a difference in Mike lately. Even he thinks this is it," Debbie said with a hint of sadness.

"Wow, so it's not just me? I truly feel like I have gone to heaven. I never knew it could be like this. No fights. We are on the same page. I feel like I must be dreaming. It's just all too good to be true, especially for me!"

"Well, it *is* true, and I am so happy for you! I think Ryan and I will never be more than friends but we still have a great time hanging out," Debbie remarked.

The boys came back to the table and we obviously had to stop our chatter about them. The rest of the night was filled with laughter. Ryan had a really good sense of humor. I felt bad that things weren't working out exactly as I hoped for him and my cousin. We stayed until the place closed. We said goodbye to Ryan and Debbie and got in the car.

"If ten years from now, we can talk this much and feel this way, I think it would be like heaven," Mike spoke softly.

"I feel the same. I can't believe it hasn't even been a month, yet I feel like I have known you forever."

"That's what happens when you talk to someone for how many hours now, a hundred?" he replied with a laugh.

Words of love were not spoken, maybe out of fear from both of us since it seemed maybe too soon to believe it was love. I thought after that there was such a thing as love at first sight, but I didn't say it. We sat in the car for four hours talking. It was after six in the morning when I finally made my way up the stairs to my room. We hated saying goodbye.

On November 22nd, less than a month since we'd met, Mike said the magic words to me.

"I have never felt this way before in my life! You are the best thing to ever happen to me. I love you," Mike stated as he gazed deeply into my eyes.

"I love you too! I have been dying to say that but wasn't sure you felt the same," I replied like a giddy teenager.

"I've been wanting to say it for a long time now, but…wasn't sure how you were going to feel if I said it too soon," Mike admitted hesitantly.

"No, we are completely on the same page here, thank God!" I replied in a relieved voice.

He pulled me close to him, took me in his arms, and surrounded me in love and kisses.

"I'm going to miss you until I see you again, you know that, right?" he whispered. "I really hate saying goodbye, it seems to get harder each time I see you."

"I know, now we have to go two days until we see each other again. Wish you didn't have to work," I teased him.

"I'll call you as soon as I get home each night," he promised. "I'm sure we'll wind up talking for hours, so the two days will go fast...Love you, just had to say it again, now that it's out there."

The next two days did drag somewhat but he was right—our talking for hours each night did help the nights to at least go quickly, but the days at work seemed to drag.

Then I finally got to see him.

"I have a surprise for you," he taunted with a huge grin on his face.

"Tell me."

"We're going into the city to see the Christmas tree and go on a horse and buggy ride." His excitement was contagious.

"Are you serious?"

"Let's go. I already have our train tickets." He pulled the tickets out of his pocket.

The night was beyond magical. The Christmas tree. The smells of chestnuts. All the stores decorated. Going on a horse and buggy ride. All of it was so amazing I didn't want it to end. We found someone to take our picture for us in front of the tree. I looked at him and couldn't imagine a life without him. I imagined my eyes were as bright as those Christmas tree lights we'd just seen.

We spent the rest of December as inseparable as we could be, based on our jobs. We shopped and wrapped presents. We visited friends and family and went to Christmas parties. In such a short time, I felt as if my whole life had changed.

Then we spent Christmas day at my house for dinner. My whole family loved him and had completely welcomed him. He gave me a bunch of Islander things, leading me to think they were my only gifts. Later, when we were alone, he handed me a beautiful double-heart ring. We went to his house for dessert and spent some time with family. It had been such a wonderful Christmas and I truly didn't want the day to end.

~* * * *~

Mike worked New Year's Eve, so I went out with Debbie and Ryan, and we met a bunch of other people at Copperwaites. It wasn't very fun for me, like when Mike was around.

Debbie pulled me aside as soon as Ryan was distracted with our other friends. "I have to tell you something and I don't think you're going to be happy when I do," she whispered in a voice that scared me.

"What does it have to do with?" I said as I got that sinking feeling in my stomach, wondering what on earth was wrong. So many things went running through my mind.

"Mike told Ryan that you are smothering him," Debbie said softly.

"WHAT, are you serious? What the hell does that mean? I haven't smothered him! We haven't even had a fight. This makes no sense whatsoever. Are you sure that Ryan wasn't just making this up?" I asked, convinced this was a mistake.

"I don't think Ryan would lie about something like that. I wasn't supposed to say anything but you know I had to tell you."

"I just don't get it, and what am I supposed to do now? If I say something, then Ryan will find out you told me and I don't want to get you in trouble." I was getting very upset but trying to hold it in.

"Cas, you're my cousin first and foremost. If you have to say something and Ryan gets mad at me then so be it. You are more important to me and I feel horrible about this. It doesn't make sense to me either. I have seen you two together. I have seen the way he looks at you, I know he loves you."

"I just don't know what to do. I want to get out of here. I couldn't even talk to Mike if I wanted to tonight. My heart just smashed into a million pieces, but until I find out why and even if he said that, how am I supposed to act normal?"

"I am so sorry, Cas. I really am!"

HAPPY NEW YEAR! There were the usual noises of ringing in a new year, with horns, yelling, and kissing, as total chaos began to fill the bar. It was 1987. A new year and once again, I didn't feel like any of it was real.

CHAPTER FOURTEEN

1987 – Age 24

I didn't know how to process what I'd heard. I was afraid to say anything to Mike, afraid of what he might say. Nothing seemed to be making sense. We didn't even fight. I didn't understand why it was happening to me. I was so happy and had every reason to believe that he felt the same. I didn't understand; what changed?

When Mike picked me up to go out, I decided to not say anything just yet. I would just see how he acted and what he said.

It didn't take long during the drive to realize that something was clearly different. That look of love in his eyes no longer seemed to be there. I was sitting with a million questions reeling through my mind as I tried to figure out when he was going to drop the bomb on me. My brain said to not open my mouth but my heart decided it had to. "What is going on?" I quietly asked.

"Nothing."

"You're not acting the way you used to. There is something different, something has changed here," I stated harshly.

"I...um, don't know what to say."

"What the hell does that mean? Something is going on and I think that you owe me an explanation." My anger grew by the minute.

"I don't know where to start," he hesitantly said.

"How about anywhere! Just tell me what is going on."

"I'm sorry but we just can't go out any more," he blurted. "It started when my ex-girlfriend called me. I went with her for a long time. Hearing from her and talking to her made me realize that I don't want to get married now. I feel that is where we were headed if we continued to go out."

"You can't be serious! I wasn't pushing you into marriage! Everything was perfect," I cried.

"I know—that is the problem, everything was too perfect, it—kind of scared me," he said softly. "You are the marrying type and I'm not ready to get married."

"This has to be the lamest excuse for breaking up that I have ever heard! I by no means was pushing to get married and you know it! I think you just used me and wanted to get back with your ex-girlfriend! Take me home!"

"I—"

"Save it, I really don't want to hear another word!"

The rest of the ride back to my house was silent. I couldn't even cry. I was fuming. When he finally pulled in front of my house, I got out of the car the second I could. As I slammed his car door, I heard him say, "I am sorry."

I didn't want to face my parents and luckily, they were out that night. I went to my room and just sat, re-thinking all that had just happened. I was too angry to cry. I called my cousin and told her what he said.

She was just as dumbfounded as me. "Screw him! Let's just go out tomorrow night. Maybe he'll realize what he just lost and call you?" she added, sympathetically.

"Seriously, I don't know that I would trust him again after this. It seems as if everything has just been a lie or a show, nothing was genuine and real. I feel like I finally moved on with my life for the first time since losing Danny, only to find Mike didn't really love me."

I was so tired of having my heart walked on over and over again. I was going to go about my life and maybe someday, I would find that right one—maybe, maybe not. I deserved someone who could make my heart race and flutter every time I heard their voice. I wanted someone who made me feel like Danny did, whose voice was all I needed. Losing Mike made me realize that as much as I believed I loved him, maybe something was missing. It was nice having a boyfriend and not having any fights. Maybe, just maybe, I didn't really love him like I had thought and I was just going through the motions also? Or, maybe I did and this was the only way to get over the pain?

~* * * *~

I realized one day that my life was a total bore. I worked and then sat around, watched television or read a book. I went out occasionally but just didn't want to deal with any more heartache that seemed to follow me around. I went to see Kyle at the bar once in a while. We talked, flirted, and went our separate ways. Nothing changed and maybe it was better that way for the time being. I also found myself thinking of Danny and missing him.

Debbie and I decided to plan a trip to Acapulco. We needed to get away from home for a while. We planned to leave on April 27, and we wouldn't come back until May 4. We would just lie in the sun and get a nice tan every day.

As the trip was getting closer, I was getting more anxious to be away. I was daydreaming when I heard the phone ring once. Maybe I imaged it? Then the phone began to ring again. It couldn't be after all those months! "Hello," I answered, my heart already racing and not even knowing if it was really Danny on the other end of the phone.

"Hey, it's me."

I couldn't believe it was him. It'd been so long since I had heard his voice. Why did just a few words send my mind racing back in time? "How are you doing? I can't believe it's really you. It has been so long since we talked." I was smiling for the first time in so long.

"I'm doing well, how are you doing?"

"I'm doing okay...I guess. My cousin and I are going away next week to Acapulco. I can't wait to get away from here for a week."

"I'm working nights at the taxi, driving a cab. You should stop by one night, say hello. Wait, what times are your flights?" he asked.

"We leave at 10:00 am on the 27th and we come home at 11:00 pm on May 4th, why?" I questioned, already praying he would say he would drive us to the airport.

"Well, I can pick you up when you come back if you want? I work nights. I wish I could drive you there too, but I have to work during the day with my dad."

"Okay, that sounds good. I have a ride to the airport, but now no one will have to come pick us up late. That will help us out a lot. Thank you!" I truly couldn't wait to see him.

"Okay, I better get back to work. It was good talking to you. I love you and I still miss you. I think of you often!"

"I love and miss you too! Goodbye." A sudden sadness reminded me that he would never again be mine.

"Bye, call me when you land on the 4th." Then he hung up.

I forgot I was holding the phone and only had a dial tone. It wasn't long before it started making that crazy noise when you don't hang it up. I hung up the phone as a tiny tear fell slowly down my cheek. I wiped it away. I refused to cry. A part of me would always miss him, but tears wouldn't help. I found something on television to take my mind off getting to see him again. I needed to concentrate on my trip.

~* * * *~

We landed in Acapulco at 1:30. It was about 95 degrees. We couldn't wait to get in our bathing suits and go swimming. We had a beautiful oceanfront room. As fast as we could find our suits in our bags, we were dressed and ready to hit the pool. We sat in the sun and swam the rest of the afternoon. Our first night, we went to a club called *Le Dome* and had a fantastic time. We had a few drinks and danced the night away.

The next day, we sat by the pool all day. It had a slide that was so much fun. During the afternoon, we did some shopping. The prices were great! After dinner, we found another club to try, this one called Jackie O's, but they did not have a good crowd. We began to feel very out of place but wanted to dance. We should have left when we got the bad feeling. We saw some guy with a gun and quickly left. We went back to our room and watched a movie. We would never go back to that place. We would go back to *Le Dome* the next night.

We spent another day at the pool, just loving this pool. Finding good food was becoming difficult. We went out that afternoon and found a Kentucky Fried Chicken. It wasn't as bad as the rest of the food we'd been getting. We danced the night away at *Le Dome* and got back to our room at 4:00 in the morning, just in time to crash.

The next day we over-did the sun. We both were so burned and in so much pain that we felt sick. We decided to just order room service and watch television that night.

Without the pool and tanning, there wasn't much to do. We walked around downtown for a while and did some more shopping. That night we went back to *Le Dome* and danced until late. Sleep came quickly.

We made the mistake the next day of going back out in the sun and falling asleep. By the time we walked back to our room, which was very difficult, we literally were in tears. We both had blisters. Mine were on my shoulders and Debbie's were on her knees. As the night went on, the pain intensified. I'd never had a burn like that before in my life. We called downstairs, begging for help, needing something we could put on the sunburn. Nothing was open. They sent us up tomatoes. We were desperate. We sat in agony with tomatoes on our burns.

I began to think about going home. Part of me felt anxious to get back home, see my dogs, and part of me was enjoying being away from it all. I also thought what it would be like to see Danny again face to face.

Then the day to leave was upon us. When you know it's time to leave, the traveling part is annoying. You just want to get home. So, of course, our plane was delayed.

We didn't land until 1:00 am and then had to wait a long time for our luggage. I called the taxi and they said they would let Danny know we landed and that he should be there soon. He told us where to wait for him. My heart began to race, as I would see him soon, although truly I was so tired from barely any sleep and traveling all day, part of me just wanted to get home quickly.

Debbie and I were standing outside the terminal. We didn't have to wait too long. I saw a taxi and somehow I just knew it was him inside.

The taxi pulled over and he quickly got out helping us with the luggage. "You look great!" he said.

"Thanks!" As I looked at him, our eyes locked. No other words needed to be spoken. They weren't necessary.

"Hey Deb, did you have a nice trip?" he asked my cousin.

"Yeah, we could have done without the sun poisoning, but overall yes it was nice." She then laughed.

On the ride home, he asked more about what we did on vacation. We dropped my cousin off first, of course. On the way to my house, he began to tell me how much he missed me and still loved me. I of course felt the same, but it didn't change the reality. He told me to stop by and visit him at the taxi. We sat in front of my house for a while, just holding each other tight, as if we wished we would never have to let go.

"I love you, always and forever," he said with a smile.

"I love you, forever and always," I said, smiling back. It always seemed to get us to laugh, remembering the first time we said those words.

He needed to get back to work, so we shared a soft kiss on the lips that lingered and then he was gone once again.

~* * * *~

In July, around what used to be our anniversary, we arranged a night together. We drove to a fancy, romantic hotel called the Commack Motor Inn. It had a Jacuzzi in the room and a heart-shaped bed. We had stopped on the way for a bottle of champagne and I had brought two plastic cups with me. Everything about the night was magic. We were both nervous, like we'd just met, even though we had known each other for so long. The room was beautiful and cozy. We took a bubble bath together and drank some of the champagne to relax. Afterward, I changed into a nightgown I'd gotten just for that night. We made love really for the first true time. We laid side by side, our hearts pressed up to each other, beating as one. All our other times didn't have the magic that we found that night.

Time went by too fast. The magic disappeared as reality came back into our lives and we had to drive back to our lives apart. We held hands and spoke very few words for the long drive back to our other worlds. We didn't discuss when we would see each other again, as arranging time together was hard. There were no regrets, even though we both knew the night together was wrong, but the fantasy of it and opening our souls to each other would last forever.

~* * * *~

My cousin and I started going to a new nightclub we found out about. It was called Uncle Sam's. It was a really nice club and had a good crowd. The dance floor was big. Disco lights flashed and really great dancing music filled the air. When we went to the bar, we saw Bobby, Danny's friend. He was a bartender there. It was Bobby who told me that Danny's wife was having another baby, due in March. He was someone who truly believed that we would have wound up together. He thought I already knew somehow. Hearing the news broke the bubble surrounding my head, reminding me that Danny would never be mine again and that he had a family. I put on a good front and didn't show how extremely painful hearing this news truly was. I managed, with a couple drinks—at a great discount from Bobby and comforting words from my cousin—to get through the night. We had a great new place to hang out at now and life must go on. I knew the night Danny and I had together couldn't and wouldn't change anything, no matter how much I dreamed it could have. When I got home, I cried myself to sleep.

It was weeks later, when I finally visited Danny at his job. We didn't make plans to get together, we just sat and talked. I told him that I knew about the baby. He had planned to tell me, wanted to tell me, but he was afraid of how I would react. I explained to him how it hurt me deeply. How I cried myself to sleep the night I heard from Bobby, but also knew deep down what we had wasn't real. Our love was real but everything else was just a false reality. If only we were able to communicate when we were together like we were able to then. I knew I shouldn't have tortured myself by going there, but I just needed to see him even if only for a minute. I found myself thinking of him a lot.

We now had the friendship that I so wished we'd had when we were younger. We continued to talk about his life and mine. We were even able to discuss Wanda and I told him about what happened with Mike. He didn't know about Bobby bartending and wondered how I had seen him. He told me he would try to meet me there one night. I didn't stay too long and didn't want to keep him from his work. Goodbye was always the hardest part—a long hug and a quick soft kiss, until next time, if there was one.

~* * * *~

Leslie, Crystal, Liz, Debbie, and I became regulars at Uncle Sam's. Life moved forward whether I liked it or not. The girls and I had some great times, but there were times I missed having a boyfriend and there were times my thoughts were filled with Danny. It would be months later when Danny told me that he would go to Uncle Sam's to meet me and see Bobby. Everyone would be there, so in my mind it helped me to not think of the guilt of meeting behind Wanda's back.

The day our plan was supposed to happen, I woke up sick, and as much as I wanted to go, there was just no way I could. I spent the night wondering if he showed up and if he asked about me.

When I spoke to Debbie the next day she told me that he did show up and seemed disappointed that I wasn't there. I guessed the night just wasn't meant to be and hopefully one day soon, we could try to arrange it again, although it wasn't easy for him to get out and take off work. Wanda thought he was working.

Lately, all I did was get sick. My job was making me sick, being around so many people's mouths. I decided to make a change and quit. I found a job as a nanny for two little girls, close to my house, and that gave me a chance to do something totally different for a while. Maybe I just needed some changes to get me out of the rut I felt I was in.

The woman I started working for was named Debra. It was going to be confusing with two Debbie's in my life. The little girls were adorable and I loved spending time with them. I got to be outdoors. I took them for walks all over town. A part of me always hoped to pass Danny in his work van. He drove a van during the day with his job for his dad.

I filled my days with work and my nights either with one of the girls, or with all of them, or recently, getting really close to my mom. She enjoyed getting out of the house, so we found lots of excuses to go shopping. I found myself sharing many of my feelings with her, except about Danny. Maybe someday. For the time being, I was just happy to have her as a friend as well as my mother.

I also had become really close with Debra. She wasn't much older than me, so we seemed to have a lot in common. Her children loved me as I did them, and Debra was thrilled to have someone she trusted to care for them while she worked.

Danny and I met at the taxi once in a while. He tried to pass my new job and stopped by when he could for a quick hello and to see how I was doing. We didn't make any plans to see each other, other than our little meetings at his job or mine.

The holidays came and went. It was the first year that I didn't have anyone special to share them with. It was very depressing, yet I had my newfound friendship with my mom, which made them bearable. Debra and the kids also made the holidays more fun. Seeing kids' faces around the holidays always makes things brighter.

New Year's Eve, Crystal, Leslie, Liz, Debbie, and I went to Gadgets. It'd been a long time since we had gone there. It was nice to see Kyle and catch up. Even though we still had some sort of chemistry, we didn't act on it. We seemed to do better as friends. He did find me at midnight and gave me a nice hug and kiss.

My friends and I stayed until almost closing and then went to a diner on the way home for a snack. It was so late when we finally were all safely at home. Another year bit the dust.

CHAPTER FIFTEEN

1988 – Age 25

The New Year began and my somewhat boring life continued. I dreamed of being married and having kids. When I was with the little girls, it made me want to have children even more.

I found out from my parents in March when Danny's wife had the baby. His parents called mine to share the news.

I didn't try to visit him at the taxi and he didn't call for months. It would be just too hard hearing about the baby. He eventually called me and asked me to visit one night. We tried to not see each other, we tried not to care, but the minute we met, the feelings seemed to overpower us and we wanted to see each other more and more.

"Why couldn't you have been like this when we were together?" I asked Danny.

It was dark as we sat in his taxi and it was late at night. I couldn't see his eyes, and his eyes always told me a story.

"I wish I knew," he said with sadness.

Silence temporarily filled the car, but with us, words didn't seem to be needed.

He reached for my hand and we sat holding hands tightly. "I always think about you, wonder what you are doing. I know I shouldn't and I know I shouldn't still miss you...but I do," he admitted as he stared out the window.

"I don't know what to say—it is so hard not seeing you and talking to you when I want to."

"I know...but we are together right now. I know it's not the same or enough, but..." His voice trailed off. "I do love you; it's not easy for me either. But I have a family and—"

"Don't say it, please just don't, and do not remind me, not tonight," I said as my heart tightened.

I didn't stay too long because he needed to work. But the goodbyes were always hard.

Two weeks later, my phone rang late at night. Thank God, I had my own phone number. I didn't think my parents would appreciate being woken.

"It's me, sorry for calling so late. Any way you can come to my work tomorrow night?" Danny's familiar voice asked me.

I woke up instantly. His voice had that kind of power over me. "Hi, yeah, I should be able to. Is everything okay?" My inner voice was telling me something was not right; his voice sounded strange.

"We will talk tomorrow. Can you come by about midnight? I have to go, sorry to cut this so short, but I have to go pick someone up. Love you."

"Okay...love you too, bye," I said as my insides truly sensed I wasn't going to be happy about whatever was coming.

"Bye." The phone clicked off.

Did I detect a hint of something, or was it just my imagination playing tricks on me? Or was I still asleep? It was so hard to try to go back to sleep, as I laid there wondering and wishing I didn't have to wait so long to find out.

In the morning, I didn't tell anyone anything. It was so hard keeping it to myself. I wanted to talk about it, but...I didn't.

The day dragged by. I couldn't stop thoughts from running through my head. What if he had decided he wanted me back? Liz called and wanted to go out that night. I didn't tell her that I was meeting him. I agreed to go out for a while, more so to pass time more quickly.

We went to McQuade's for dinner. We found a booth and sat down. I wanted to drink but knew that I had to drive to see Danny later.

"You're acting really strange tonight," Liz noted.

"Sorry, guess it's obvious. I thought I was hiding it well," I said, laughing.

"You should know better than that! I've known you way too long to not know something is up, so spill it!"

"I really didn't want to tell anyone. I myself am not sure what it's all about." I told her about the phone call and wound up blurting out all our other secret meetings. It actually felt good to say it all and not keep it a secret. She knew about our earlier meetings, but she didn't know that we had been meeting more frequently recently.

"Um—wow! I am kind of speechless. You're setting yourself up for disaster again."

"I know—but, maybe not, maybe he is going to come back to me?" I said hopefully.

"I am your friend forever, you know that, right? But—do you really want him to leave her and his children?" Liz asked as only a best friend could bluntly tell you that you're not being smart.

Her words struck a reality in me. Did I want him to leave her for me? Did I really think it would be that easy? What would his family say? What on earth would mine? "But—I love him," I cried softly.

"I know you do, you probably always will. He was your first love and you share such a history. I'm not trying to be mean. I just don't want to see you setting yourself up to get hurt again."

"I know…and I appreciate your honesty. I just miss him and want with all my heart to go back in time." My eyes began to fill; a single tear dropped and ran slowly down my cheek.

"I don't mean to upset you. I know this whole situation is so hard for you. Let's not talk about it anymore, okay?" Liz suggested. "You know I will always be there if you need me."

I could see her genuine sadness for me. I also knew she was only telling me what someone needed to. I took a deep breath and gathered my inner strength. I couldn't go there all upset when I didn't even know why he wanted to see me.

Our food arrived and we talked about things other than Danny. We didn't stay long after we ate. We got in her car and she drove me back to my house.

"Do you want me to stay with you until it's time to go see him?" she asked.

"No, it's okay. I know you need to get up early tomorrow. I'll be okay. I promise."

"Okay, if you're sure? I'll keep the phone by my bed if you need to call me later," she said.

"Thank you! Hopefully, I won't have to call you. Goodnight." I opened the door and stepped out of the car. I made my way up the stairs and went inside. I went up to my room and thought about what she told me…hoping to have a life with someone that had married another. How wrong it was and I knew she was right. How did I get in this place in my life?

When I got in my car, my heart began to race. I felt so anxious and nervous to see him. I just wanted to be there and to know why he wanted me to come.

When I got there, his boss came over to my car and told me Danny was on a call. He said he would be there soon. When I saw his car pull in a few minutes later, my heart began to race again, and my hands instantly became sweaty.

"Hey, were you waiting long?" Danny asked as he was getting in my car.

"No, I haven't been here long," I replied, maybe too fast.

"I'm off for a couple hours. Let's go drive somewhere, okay?" he asked as he closed the door.

"Should I be worried?" I asked with a laugh, but with a hint of seriousness.

He didn't answer, but only stared out the car window.

"Now you are really scaring me!" I exclaimed, extremely scared. I drove as the silence in the car continued. I found myself driving to our familiar spot. It was by the docks, nice, peaceful, and beautiful. If it was going to be bad, then it might as well be where I got this last fateful news. I pulled over and turned the car off. I turned toward him and our eyes connected.

"I always seem to have to apologize to you. I don't want to hurt you. I really hope that you believe that," he said softly. "I have been selfish. I have made some huge mistakes, ones that I can't go back and change. It is my fault this all has happened. You didn't do anything wrong, you know that. I am the one who messed up…but I can't let my mistakes keep hurting you and holding you back from the happiness you should have. I also didn't want to let you fully go. My love for you is not like any other I have ever known. I try to move on and try to forget you, but honestly, something always happens that reminds me of you or I see something…" He paused and looked at me.

"I don't know what you expect me to say. I don't know what this is leading to. I try to get on with my life, too, but—I love you and you should have been with me!" I cried.

"I have thought about this and I want you to understand before I tell you, that I'm not doing this to hurt you. Actually, it's quite the opposite." His words hung in the air.

"Please just tell me. I do believe you wouldn't set out to hurt me. Sadly, that is what keeps happening, though, doesn't it?" I asked almost in a whisper.

"I'm going to move away. I am going to move off Long Island. Actually, we just got a place upstate."

"What?" I screamed.

"I am so sorry! I really am! This is hard for me too, but we need to get on with our lives. I can't seem to do it and you can't either. It's the only way that maybe it will work, if I move away. I need to give my marriage a try and...I just haven't fully been able to do that when I'm still thinking of and still loving you. This way, we won't be able to see each other and we can both move on, like we should have done a long time ago." Danny's voice was filled with sadness.

There was a long pause before I got the strength to say anything. We sat in silence, staring out the windows. It was so quiet I thought I could hear our heartbeats, as two hearts were ripped in two, instead of the single heart we shared not so long ago.

His words stung like a huge open cut with alcohol being poured into it. My heart hurt, my head hurt, and emptiness filled me. Yet, I knew deep down after the shock of his words ringing in my head, that he was right. "You're—right," I finally spoke as the tears racing down my cheeks began to roll down my neck. I took some deep breaths and tried to keep my composure. I needed to let him go, I knew I did. Deep down, it was the right thing to do—to finally set him free. "I've never fully been able to move on with my life. I try, but—there is always that part of me that thinks of you, loves you."

"I will never forget you...I will always love you, please never forget that." He gazed deeply into my eyes...those eyes that always turned me to Jell-O.

I had to stop looking at him. It was only making it harder, knowing this was where our story would really end.

"What we had was—is—unique," Danny mumbled.

I stared at him with tear-filled eyes. "It will be so hard," I gasped through my tears. "I always knew if I really needed you, you really weren't far away." I knew I needed to stop—I needed to not make this any harder than it already was, but the tears just wouldn't stop falling.

"Please don't cry," he said as he reached over and wiped away some tears. "You know I hate when you cry; it breaks my heart. You will find someone, I know you will, someone who will love you and treat you the way I always should have, the way you really deserved."

Through the tears, I manage to say, "I do deserve happiness and someone who can be mine all the time. Someday, some way, I will find it, but my love for you—that is forever and always. There will always be a part of me that will remember—will still think of you."

He hesitated before saying, "I know..." His voice faded away and I heard him take a deep breath. "I'm not going to call you before I leave.

I think us talking or seeing each other again, will be just too hard, this is hard enough."

"So, this is really goodbye?" Even though I knew the answer and I knew it was for the best, a part of my soul was leaving and I would never be whole again. My sobs began to get uncontrollable, as silence filled the air and my tears were all that was left.

He opened his car door, walked around to my side of the car and opened my door. He took my hand and pulled me toward him, out of the car. He took me in his arms and made me look at him. "Please…stop crying…this is so hard. You know I love you," Danny whispered as he gazed into my soul and kissed me gently.

He held me tightly until I was finally able to calm down. I didn't have words. There was so much I wanted to say, needed to say, knowing this would really be our last time together. Yet, I found myself at a total loss and knew deep down, nothing would change our reality, our destiny.

"I'll drive the car. I don't think you're in any shape to drive. I just couldn't tell you something like this over the phone, I just had to see you and tell you in person. I-I'm sorry. You will never know just how sorry I am."

I nodded my head in agreement, as our last hug and last kiss died, just like a beautiful rose when its petals whither and begin falling to the ground.

I don't remember the drive back to the taxi. I just knew it was too fast. There were no more words to say. Saying anything more at that time would only have made it worse than it already was.

He pulled over and got out of the car. He went around to my side of the car and opened my door.

I hesitated slightly before I gathered up enough strength to get out and stand.

Our eyes locked, maybe too long.

"I will love you! Always and forever!" he said.

I wanted to just feel his arms wrapped around me again, yet I knew we couldn't. It was over. The longer we dragged this out the harder it would be. "I will love you too! Forever and Always!" I whispered as my tears began to slowly roll down my cheeks.

I watched for a moment as he walked away. I walked around to get in the car and sat down. I glanced up to the rear-view mirror, wondering where he was. It was dark and I couldn't see his face but I saw his silhouette. He was watching my car as I finally put the car in drive and slowly pulled away. I looked in the mirror until he faded and was gone from my sight. Our love was now just a memory.

CHAPTER SIXTEEN

Six months later

"Kyle and Eric should be here soon, you almost ready?" Leslie questioned.

I was fumbling around in the bathroom, putting the finishing touches on my makeup. "They should be here soon," I repeated, laughing, because I knew she was so impatient to see Eric again. We were smart in setting her up with him; they got along really well.

"I really like his friend," I heard her echo through the door.

A huge smile filled my face as I remembered how much she seemed to light up when we introduced them to each other.

"Have I told you lately how happy I am that you and Kyle worked things out and decided to give it another chance?" Her enthusiastic voice filled the air.

"I know, me too." I glanced at my own reflection and saw a glimmer of light behind my once-darkened eyes.

My mind began to wander and I had an imaginary conversation with Kyle:

"You look really great tonight!" I haven't seen you in so long, how is everything?" Kyle asks.

"I am doing great! Been really busy with work and getting some things straightened out in my life, but I am good, really good." Maybe for the first time in a long time, I think to myself.

"Do you think you could hang out until I get off? We can go talk and catch up?" he questions.

"Sure, that would be really nice. It really has been a long time." A smile fills my face, something I haven't been able to do for a long time. It had been six months since that fateful night that turned me upside down.

"I have missed seeing you. Okay, let me get back to work and we will talk later," he said as he moved away, smiling. He needed to get drinks for people who'd been patiently waiting while he chatted with me.

I walk away and find my friends. I tell them that I'm going to stay and go out with Kyle after he gets off. I think they smiled even brighter than me.

I find him gazing at me the rest of the night as I dance until I can no longer feel my feet. The time goes by really quickly and before I know it, he is finally off work.

We get into his car. Winter is starting, so it's really cold. We sit in his car waiting for it to warm up.

"I really am glad you decided to come tonight," he says.

"Me too, it was a lot of fun. I haven't danced so much, in so long," I say, laughing.

We drive to my house, but sit in his car for hours, catching up. Having known each other and being together on and off for the last ten years, talking comes easy for us.

"I want to take you out. Are you free tomorrow night?" he asks.

"Yeah, I would like that," I answer, thinking this feels right, this feels really right.

He leans over, gives me a soft, quick kiss and a hug.

I open the door and get out of the car.

"I will pick you up at 7:00, okay?"

"Sounds perfect, see you tomorrow, or should I say later?" I laugh, realizing it is already morning, as I close the car door.

I walk into my house and make my way to my room, completely exhausted, yet exhilarated at the same time. It takes me a while to fall asleep and I don't wake until the afternoon. It takes me the rest of the day to figure out what to wear tonight.

When he picks me up at 7:00, he tells me that he couldn't stop thinking about me all day.

Actually, he wished he had said he was coming earlier. He drives us to a nice restaurant.

We sit at a table and I look at him across the table.

He is staring at me, very deep in thought. "I shouldn't have ever let you go." His words ring in my ears. "I don't want to risk losing you again. Will you please go out with me again?"

"Yes!" I say as I am filled with a feeling that I thought would never be a part of my life again.

"Will you hurry up; they are going to be here."

Leslie's words broke into my daydreaming. "Okay, sorry. I was just thinking. I'm ready." I took one last glance in the mirror to see how I looked, and then I heard the doorbell ringing.

The next two months with Kyle were nothing less than perfect. For the first time in our history, we really seemed to be on the same page. Since my family already knew him, and his family knew me, we fell back into each other's lives so easily.

~* * * *~

"Merry Christmas," Kyle said as he handed me a tiny box.

The room was filled with presents everywhere. The Christmas tree lights were glistening in his eyes as he watched me closely while I took the box from his hands.

"Merry Christmas," I replied as I opened the box. Inside was a beautiful heart ring with our initials engraved on it. "Oh, my God…I love it!" I exclaimed as I quickly put it on my hand. I leaned over and kissed him. I got up and found his present. I got him a really nice watch, which coincidentally was also engraved with our initials on the back of it.

"I love it!" he said as he put it on.

"You're a hard one to buy for. I'm so glad you like it. I love my ring!" I knew I was beyond beaming with happiness.

We spent dinner with my family and dessert with his. Everyone loved my ring and he got a lot of nice compliments on his new watch.

"I'm sorry I can't get off New Year's Eve," he said sadly. "You know I would if I could, but you will come there with your friends, right?"

"Of course! I wouldn't want to be anywhere else. We'll go out the next night. It's fine, seriously," I said, wishing he could have had the night off, but I knew taking off New Year's when you work in a bar wasn't an easy task.

~* * * *~

The club looked very crowded. It was so hard to even get near the bar to see Kyle. Every time I made my way to the bar and had to stand a long time, waiting for his attention, he apologized. With the place so packed when it was almost midnight, I couldn't even see him through the crowd and felt sad that I wouldn't get to kiss him. Of course, I did understand—it was his job.

Then when midnight arrived and the noise was so loud, it felt as if the lights would come crashing down, he found me.

"Aren't you going to get in trouble for leaving the bar?" I asked, although I was so happy to have him standing next to me.

"Don't worry about it, I took care of it. I can only stay for a minute, but I couldn't let the New Year begin without you," he said lovingly, as he put his hands on my cheeks and gave me a kiss. "Happy New Year. I love you." He gazed deep into my eyes.

"Happy New Year to you, too, and I love you, too," I said, gazing deeply into his eyes as 1988 ended and a New Year began with happiness.

I got home really late, or should I say, early in the morning. It was a great night even though I didn't fully get to spend it with Kyle. When I finally crawled into bed, I found myself thinking of Danny. I don't know what triggered it. It had been so long since I had even let him cross my mind. A part of me just wished I knew if he was really happy and if he was okay. Maybe it was because I believed I was finally happy and okay. It'd been a long, hard road but I made it. I was finally at a place where I could feel happiness for him and his life without me and me without him. I loved him still, I would always love him, and I would always deep down, miss him. I found a way to shake the thoughts away and finally drifted off to sleep, dreaming of my night ahead with Kyle.

CHAPTER SEVENTEEN

1989 – Age 26

Six months later......

"Can you believe we have been together almost a year?" I asked, excited that maybe one day soon, he would surprise me with an engagement ring. At least I hoped.

"I know, it seems like just yesterday," Kyle responded.

I kept thinking of my clock ticking. I saw time passing too fast. I just wanted to be married. I wanted children while I was still young. I hinted every chance I got to get the message across to him. I even spoke to his sister about it and she thought he was just not ready to make that kind of commitment. It was becoming very frustrating. I tried not to harp about it but on the inside, my frustration began to take on an anger towards him at times.

He saw the look in my eyes and, knowing me so well, he knew what I was thinking. "I am sorry…I'm just not ready for what you're thinking."

"How do you know what I'm thinking?" I asked, even though I knew he was right.

"I know you. I don't have the type of job I need to have to support a family. I am content with what we have for now. I wish you were able to feel the same."

"I am content, I just—want to have a family and sometimes, I think maybe you will never want the same thing," I responded.

"I can't answer that for sure right now," he explained. "I know I love you and I want to be with you, but marriage just isn't something I am ready to do just now. I can't say when that might change, if it will change."

"It would just be nice to know that we do have a future together," I whined. I just kept hearing that word *IF* over and over in my head.

Kyle had no answers or explanations. We tried hard and did manage to temporarily move past it, but it continued to be a constant thorn in our sides.

Since we knew each other so well and really did care about each other, we decided it would be best if we spent some time apart. There was no hate. There were no ugly words between us, and there were no tears. We both felt sad, but we just couldn't seem to get on that same page about a future together. Maybe time apart would show him what I meant to him.

Maybe it was just the push that he needed to make that final commitment to me.

~* * * *~

I found a new routine alone and found myself really enjoying my time with my mother. My relationship with her was unlike what my friends had with their moms. I loved spending time with her. We went shopping, watched movies in my room, and went to hockey games on the nights my dad didn't feel like going. They purchased season tickets since we all loved going so much. I knew my parents' marriage wasn't the happiest and when my mom was with me, she seemed happy. I felt lucky to have the closeness I did with her.

At work, Debra was having another baby soon, so I would have three children to take care of. I didn't mind, it just pulled my heart strings. I was hoping that someday, it would be me having a baby. I dreamed of having a married life and a home I could call my own.

~* * * *~

My parents decided we were going to go to Nashville, Tennessee. Country music had always been a part of my life. It would be a family vacation for all of us. We hadn't really ever had a family vacation, so this was something new and exciting.

The trip changed everything for us as a family. When you're older, you begin to see your parents in a totally different light than when you were younger. My dad was a lot of fun on vacation. He was much less OCD when he was away. It reminded me of a time when I was younger, when I was really close to him. I was a total daddy's little girl and would stand talking to him every day when he shaved. Once I hit those teen years and then boys came into my life, we grew apart.

Being in Tennessee together helped us to become the family that we hadn't been in years. We stayed in the most beautiful hotel I'd ever seen in my life, Opryland. It had waterfalls inside. Everything about it was wonderful.

We met my parents' family friends there, Norman and Helen. I had known them my whole life. They were the funniest people to be around, not even trying to be. We didn't know it originally, but Norman had sleep apnea and everywhere we went he fell asleep. We went to the Grand Ole Opry show, during which he fell asleep and spilled his drink all over the girl in front of him. At a concert, he fell asleep, and during a silent part was snoring loudly as everyone in the stadium looked our way. At the NASCAR stock car races, someone clammed him.

Norman loved to bust my dad's chops about his OCD. My dad took many medications, most of them vitamins and some prescriptions necessary for his health. They were all laid out on the bed as my dad was organizing them. Norman decided to put on a pair of Doctor Dentins with feet, came running into our room—their room was attached—and jumped on the bed, sending the pills flying everywhere. Under normal circumstances, my dad would have completely lost it. This time, however, there was can't-even-breathe-holding-your-stomach laughter.

Time away always goes by way too fast, but we talked about going back there again really soon. I saw my parents in a whole new light during that vacation. We even talked of the possibility of moving to Tennessee someday, when they retired.

I found myself on a completely new path of life. A life where my family had taken on a whole new meaning and where spending time enjoying life with them was actually something I looked forward to doing more of.

~* * * *~

My parents arranged for us to go back to Tennessee for Country Christmas. While we were in Tennessee before, we had heard that Country Christmas was the best. That gave me something to look forward to for the holiday season, since I didn't have anyone special to share it with that year, at least as of that time.

The week in Tennessee during Christmas was amazing! Everywhere we went, there were beautiful lights and people singing. I found myself in a Christmas spirit that I never dreamed I would have that year. My dad was such a different person on vacation and I found that time with my parents was a time to cherish. We made such wonderful memories and shared many laughs.

I found myself at night thinking of Danny and wishing he could be there with me to see all of it. He would have loved it there.

My relationship with my parents was different now after sharing those trips. I found myself treated more like the adult that I was, rather than the child they always tried to protect, especially my dad. My mom and I had already developed a mature, respectable friendship. She became a best friend I could turn to when I needed, as well as being my mother who wanted to protect me. Now, my dad had also become someone I could relate to in a whole different way, and instead of resenting time, I looked forward to more times together.

Christmas Day was an uneventful but wonderful time with my parents and grandparents. I didn't make any plans like usual, to go out and get away from them. I was perfectly content just being home.

On New Year's Eve, my parents were planning a really big party at our house. A lot of people would be there, family and my parents' friends. I convinced my cousin to be there instead of going out. For the first time since we were kids, we would stay home on New Year's Eve and ring it in with family.

"Are you sure you are going to be okay with Danny's parents here tonight?" Debbie asked me.

"I'm fine, seriously! I doubt with me around, they will even mention his name."

"I know you are fine, but—"

"There are no buts. I'm looking forward to the party and not worried at all about seeing his parents. It has been a really long time. I'm a different person now, you know that." She knew all the past tears, hard days, and hard nights I endured, which gave me the strength I now had. "It's also going to be really strange not being at Gadgets tonight. I wonder if Kyle will even think of me?"

"You're right, wow. I didn't even think of that one," Debbie replied. "I've just been worried about Danny's parents. I didn't even realize this will be your first New Year's in two years, you won't be at Gadgets."

"This will be a totally different start of a new year. I'm really looking forward to a year that maybe starts and actually ends happy," I said. "No more tears, only good things to come, and maybe this will be the year of great things for me, for once, and for you!"

"Yes! Tonight we will begin a New Year and this will be a great year for both of us, finally!" Debbie added enthusiastically. "Next week, let's go to Gillie's. Maybe we'll meet some New York Islanders. One of my friends says a bunch of them go there after the games now."

"That sounds good to me!"

I didn't share my inner thoughts with anyone of Danny that day, or my true thoughts about not being at Gadgets that night. I didn't want to go there. I just wondered what, if anything, would Kyle think when I didn't show up. Even though I hadn't talked to him in a while, I bet he thought I would show up. The last time he called me late one night, he was hinting for me to go down and visit soon. I would go there one night soon, but for now, I was really happy just being home with my family. I also did worry about seeing Danny's parents, even though I did believe they wouldn't discuss him around me. But seeing them always

brought back memories. I was stronger now
though, and I thought deep down I would get
through the night with flying colors. Even
though I'd been hurt so many times, I wouldn't
change anything about my past. I had no regrets.
My destiny would find its way to me someday.

~* * * *~

We set up the house for the New Year
party. We hung banners and lights all around.
Everyone started arriving around 8.00 pm.
My dad put some good music on the stereo.
Laughter, conversation, and music began to fill
my house. When Danny's parents arrived, as
luck would have it, I was the one who opened
the door. There was no awkwardness, which I
had pictured in my mind as a possibility. They
seemed genuinely happy to see me, even gave
me a great big hug and kiss. It put me at ease
and set the stage for a great evening ahead.

A short while later in the kitchen, as we got
some of the food to serve, my mom stopped me.

"You okay?" she asked. She knew this was
the first time I'd been face to face with Danny's
parents in a long time.

"Yes, I'm fine, really! You sound like
Debbie," I said, laughing.

"I am proud of you and I'm really glad that you're here tonight," my mom said with a look of deep love in her eyes.

"Me too mom, me too. I love you!"

"I love you, too," she said with a huge smile.

My parents didn't spare anything for that night. At midnight, tons of horns and noisemakers filled my house with the wonderful sounds of celebration.

When everyone left, we all pitched in and cleaned up the best we could before crashing.

That night was the perfect beginning to what I envisioned to be a perfect year ahead. For a brief second, I thought of Danny as sleep took over.

CHAPTER EIGHTEEN

1990 – Age 27

"Oh, my God! I can't believe we're actually going out with New York Islanders tonight!" Debbie giggled. "I still can't believe this happened."

"I know. I can't believe we are either!" I said ecstatically.

We'd met them on our first official New Year weekend out. We went to Gillie's to watch the hockey game. A couple of hours after the game, the players started piling in. The place was packed. We just happened to have extra chairs at our table and two of them asked if we minded if they sat with us. Who were we to say no to two hockey players? We knew a lot about hockey, so talking to them was pretty easy, and they did like to talk about themselves. They asked to take us to dinner the following night and we both immediately agreed. We didn't have any high expectations about seeing them again. We just really thought it would be cool to say we went out with them.

The next night, we met the guys at the restaurant. It was a really nice place, fancy and quiet, and with soft lights. It didn't seem to take long before Debbie and I realized just how truly self-centered they really were. In the bathroom, we both laughed hysterically about it, but we knew someday, we would be able to say we went on a date with them and that made it all worthwhile. I thought we bored them and we weren't surprised at the end of the night when they didn't mention getting together again. We spent the car ride home laughing about our memorable evening.

The following weekend we went back to Gillie's. We did see them there and they were polite and at least said, "Hi," to us, but we didn't sit with them.

~* * * *~

My phone rang late one night. I was half asleep as I reached for it.

"It's me," he said.

My heart stopped for an instant and I woke up. He didn't need to say his name—I knew his voice. "How are you?" I asked as my mind took me back in time. It'd had been so very long since I heard his voice. I hadn't talked to him at all since that night we said goodbye and I watched him disappear from my life.

"I'm doing good," he replied.

We made small talk for a few minutes. He then began to tell me about how big the baby was and how he was driving a bus for a hotel.

I told him about my life. I told him about my vacations to Tennessee with my parents, and my job. He got really quiet when I told him about the hockey player.

"Sounds like you are doing good and are happy," he remarked.

"Yes, I really am. It has been a long hard road, but yes I can say with all honesty that I am happy and content with my life," I stated with complete confidence in my words. "By the way, I saw your parents a couple of weeks ago. They were here for New Year's."

"I was afraid to call you. I really didn't want to think about you meeting someone new, I know it's wrong. I wasn't even sure if you maybe even got engaged or something."

"No, I am not engaged." I laughed. "I hope someday, but for now, I'm content with my life the way it is. I am enjoying hanging out with my cousin."

"I hope me calling is all right?" he asked. "I will just feel better now, knowing that you're doing good and are really happy."

"It's fine, I'm glad that you called, really…I'm fine and I came to terms with reality a long time ago. It has been so long since we last talked, longest in all the years I have known you."

"Like I said, I didn't want to hurt you by calling. I was afraid to, but I am glad I did," he added.

"I am glad you did too," I said, as I realized I could finally handle hearing his voice and not break into tears.

We made more small talk. We didn't discuss talking to each other again.

"I better go, but it was really nice hearing your voice," he stated.

"It was really good to hear yours, too. It's nice to hear your life is happy, which is all I ever wanted for you," I said with a tiny hint of sadness, yet I smiled at the same time, while I realized just how strong I had become.

"I want you to be happy too, and I do hope you find someone that gives you all you need," he mumbled. "Bye."

"Bye," I replied as the phone call ended and I was left with a dial tone.

I felt so proud of myself about how well I thought I handled hearing his voice. I had truly moved on and that night confirmed it for me. Hearing his voice did bring back so many memories, but for the first time I was able to relive some of those memories with some happiness now. I could never regret my love for him and I knew it would never die. He would always be a part of my soul, and no matter where he was, a part of him would forever live on with me. Being able to accept that was half my battle in getting on with my life.

I didn't tell anyone about the call. I didn't want anyone getting the wrong idea. I knew the truth and I knew it was nothing more than a simple call between friends who once loved, still do, but in ways that will never be expressed again, and ways many would never understand. It was the first time we ended a conversation without saying 'I love you,' other than when we were fighting. We both now knew life was good for each other, and maybe deep down we just needed that confirmed. Although, between us, my heart never raced with anyone else the way it did when I heard Danny's voice, saw his face, or had him near me. Maybe it never would.

~* * * *~

My cousin and I continued to be regulars at Gillie's. We watched all the games that we could there. After a while, we met two guys from the team the New York Islanders played, the Buffalo Sabres. They asked Debbie if she could drop them off at their hotel nearby. It didn't cross our minds that she had a Pinto and those guys were both over six feet tall.

Watching them get in the car was nothing short of hysterical. Like something you would see in a cartoon. One guy got his hair caught on the sun visor. That was reason for all of us to get hysterical about it, even though I thought it really hurt him. Even he laughed. Their hotel wasn't far and it only took a few minutes to get there and drop them off. We didn't exchange any numbers. We knew they were leaving the next day. There was no way we would ever see them again, but we would never forget that night.

When I got back into the front seat, I could see the dark clump of hair the guy had lost and hysteria took over. Debbie had to pull over for a few minutes because she was laughing so hard, she couldn't even drive. I was going to take it off the visor when Debbie told me, "No, leave it, this way it will remind us about tonight and how much fun it was."

Even though it was somewhat late, we decided to stop in Gadgets on the way home. We were both so wide awake by then. So, we turned the car around and headed there.

I spotted Kyle behind the bar instantly. It'd been a while since I had seen him.

It didn't take him long to see me and a smile filled his face. "Hey, I was just thinking about you. You look great, by the way," he stated. "Why didn't you come here New Year's? I was watching for you all night."

"Thanks, sorry, Debbie and I just decided to stay home and spend New Year's with family this year. It was actually really nice."

"You look different for some reason," he said.

"Different? I don't know how to take that." I laughed.

"I don't know how to explain it, you just seem different," he added.

"Maybe I am. Is that a good thing?" I asked jokingly.

"Yeah, it is. Are you hanging out for a bit?"

"We will be here for a bit. I want to dance. It's been a long time," I said as I walked away to find Debbie, who was talking to two nice-looking guys.

Am I really different? Maybe, I am. I have made complete peace without Danny and Kyle. Danny touched my heart and soul in a way that will last my whole life. He will always be what I consider my soul mate. Kyle also showed me love in a totally different way. I learned I can love someone else and be loved just the same. I'm just done with being hurt and setting myself up for heartache.

Debbie and I danced and hung out with the guys she met. The guy she had in mind for me wasn't my type, though I wasn't even sure what my type was anymore. But I acted polite because Debbie clearly liked the other one. It was the least I could do.

A short while later, she pulled me aside where they couldn't hear. "You okay? Was it hard seeing Kyle?" Debbie asked.

"You know what? It really wasn't."

"He keeps watching you," she noted.

"He had his chance, he didn't want a commitment and he doesn't want marriage. I don't see that changing. I won't waste anymore of my life on someone there is no future with. I'll still be his friend," I stated in a somewhat firm voice.

"Okay...I was just asking." She laughed. "So, what do you think of John and Glenn?"

"Sorry, I didn't mean that to sound snippy, I just can't anymore, I have to live in the present. As for John and Glenn, well— umm...Glenn is not really my type but if you really like John, it's fine for tonight."

We hung out with John and Glenn until almost closing when we finally decided it was time to leave. Many times while we were there, I could sense that I was being stared at but I refused to let it bother me. "Just give me a minute. I need to say goodbye to Kyle. I'll meet you out front," I said as I headed toward the bar where Kyle was.

Dear God, please don't let Glenn ask for my number. I kept thinking.

"Okay, we'll wait out front," Debbie replied as the three of them headed toward the door.

"We're heading out. It was nice seeing you," I said to Kyle.

"You too, well I barely got to even talk to you," Kyle stated.

"Sorry, but Deb really likes this guy she met and I didn't want to leave her alone with them," I replied.

"Maybe next time…I thought maybe you were going to wait for me to get off," he muttered.

"It will only make things worse if I do that. We're in a good place right now, let's just leave it that way, so no one gets hurt," I said, shocking myself with my newfound confidence.

"Okay," he replied, but I saw sadness fill his face.

"Goodnight." I reached over, gave him a quick kiss, walked away, and didn't even look back.

"Bye," I heard him say.

By the time I got outside, I saw that John and Glenn had left. I sighed in relief that I wouldn't have to tell Glenn that I didn't want to exchange numbers.

My cousin must have seen the look of relief on my face when I didn't see them. "He knew," she said with a laugh.

"Thank God! Sorry, John might be really nice but Glenn—just not my type."

"It's fine. We will see if John even calls me. Tonight was so much fun anyway," she said as she got in the car.

I got in on my side and laughter took over again when I saw the hair on the visor, which started Debbie's hysteria again as well.

It took a little time to calm down enough for her to consider driving. "Everything go okay with Kyle?" she asked as we finally were on our way home.

"Yeah, it did. He seemed disappointed that I wasn't waiting for him to get off, but no point in setting myself up again, for a dead-end relationship."

"You have changed and you're right. Why waste any more time on him if he doesn't want what you do?"

"I guess I have changed, but I think for the best," I said softly as I gazed out the window and realized just how far I'd finally come.

When we finally pulled up at my house, we wound up laughing again at the hair. I thought that night would be a funny story we would always remember and tell everyone about.

CHAPTER NINETEEN

It seems to happen in life that just when you feel everything is going as it should, something happens that will forever change your path, your destiny. It happens so quickly— a mere heartbeat in time. Most times, you don't see it coming, so there is no preparing for it.

It started as a simple typical day. I was off work and my mom and I went shopping at the mall. Summer was just around the corner and we wanted to get some new clothes for the upcoming season. We had a great time and we laughed hard as we tried on things that we wound up thinking we would look ridiculous in. We stopped for lunch at our favorite mall restaurant when our arms couldn't carry much more. We enjoyed a nice lunch together, talked and laughed about our day. It was the perfect way to spend my day off. We finally made our way home hours later, our hands filled with bags from our purchases.

"Do you girls think you left anything in the stores for others to buy?" my dad jokingly asked us.

"Maybe, I don't know…probably not," I laughed as I glanced at my mom and smiled.

"I guess I am out of luck on getting any dinner now that you girls ate at the mall, I bet?" My dad already knew the answer. It wasn't often my mom and I went to the mall without stopping at the restaurant where we loved to eat.

"Mom will make you a nice bowl of cereal," I said, laughing as I picked up my bags and started to head upstairs to my room to put them away. After I tried them on again, of course.

"Gee, thanks," my dad said as I heard both him and my mom laughing now in the kitchen.

Then the doorbell rang.

"I got it," I said as I put the bags down on a nearby chair and walked to the door. "Are you expecting anyone?"

"No," I heard my mom say just as I put my hand on the doorknob and opened the door.

My heart stopped. I couldn't move and I was left completely speechless. If anyone would have told me what was about to happen I would never have believed them. There he was at my door, standing on my steps—and here to see me?

Why?

Our eyes locked and my mind began to fill with so many questions.

I opened the door very slowly. Our eyes continued to stay locked, I didn't even blink. I was afraid if I did that it would be a dream. My heart began to race in anticipation as I stepped outside.

We were face to face. There was nothing between us then, only unanswered questions as to what brought him to my doorstep.

"Can we talk?" he asked, not taking his eyes off mine.

"Mom, will things get better?" My daughter's words bring me back to the present, all these years later.

"Sweetheart, I wish I could say that they definitely will. Sometimes, I am afraid it's only the beginning."

About the Author

Cindy Springsteen lives on Long Island with her husband and two children. She has had a passion for writing since she was in her teens, starting with poetry, which won her numerous awards and which were published in various publications. She has spent many years researching and writing about parenting teenagers for many publications. She is presently a virtual assistant for a well-known author. This is her first novel, which is based on a true story.

Other Works by Cindy Springsteen:

Award winning *Waffles and Pancakes* Series:

Waffles and Pancakes: A Lesson in Friendship

Waffles and Pancakes: A Lesson in Bullying; Best Children's Book 2012

Waffles and Pancakes: A Lesson in the True Meaning of Christmas; Best Animal Book 2014

CPSIA information can be obtained
at www.ICGtesting.com
Printed in the USA
BVOW03s1043171217
503035BV00001B/91/P